"Dr. Amo... by our sho... offended so...

Accusing my sister of ulterior motives, indeed! And to think only a few moments ago, I thought you rather dashing!" Lifting her skirt ever so slightly with a quick motion to emphasize her rage, Lavonia turned to exit. Before she reached the doorway, the doctor's voice stopped her.

"If you do intend to work on the mission field, Miss Penn, I recommend you review the Scriptures on control of the tongue."

Turning her head in his direction, she saw a look of amusement on his countenance that made her huff with exasperation. "I assure you, Dr. Amory, I *am* controlling my tongue! Good day!"

TAMELA HANCOCK MURRAY is a Virginia native who is blessed with a wonderful husband and two daughters. She enjoys writing both contemporary and historical Christian romances. Her family activities include church youth group, Girl Scouts, choir, vacation Bible school, and Bible study. Tamela is a regular at step aerobics class and likes to exercise on the Stairmaster because she can read a book at the same time.

Books by Tamela Hancock Murray

HEARTSONG PRESENTS
HP213—Picture of Love

Don't miss out on any of our super romances. Write to us at the following address for information on our newest releases and club information.

Heartsong Presents Readers' Service
PO Box 719
Uhrichsville, OH 44683

Destinations

Tamela Hancock Murray

Heartsong Presents

A note from the author:
I love to hear from my readers! You may correspond with me
by writing: **Tamela Hancock Murray**
Author Relations
PO Box 719
Uhrichsville, OH 44683

ISBN 1-58660-072-9

DESTINATIONS

All Scripture quotations are taken from the King James Version of
the Bible.

Cover illustration by Victoria Lisi and Julius.

PRINTED IN THE U.S.A.

one

"I am so grateful to be here, Helen," Lavonia remarked over afternoon tea. "I could not bear to stay in Dover and witness the sale of everything I know on earth."

Sighing, Lavonia looked out over the Syms country estate. An unbroken carpet of grass led to a forest of swaying trees. Beyond them she could see the cool blue sky. Unbeknownst to her hostess, Lavonia had already established a habit of taking her morning devotions from her perch on a comfortable wicker chair. The time of silence, uninterrupted except for chirping birds, was ideal for contemplation.

"I am pleased to be here for you in your time of distress," Helen answered. "It is fortunate your father asked Uncle Joseph to be the executor of his will. At least you don't have to trouble yourself with such things."

"Uncle Joseph is smart with finances. He boasted to me that his fortune has grown fourfold."

"Perhaps he can put his knowledge to good use for you and Katherine," Helen speculated.

"It matters not. Without Mama and Father, the house is nothing more to me than bricks and mortar." A breeze blew one of Lavonia's curls into her eyes. She brushed the offending strand away with a delicate motion. "And it is much larger than two sisters living alone would ever need."

"The two of you together could maintain it, could you not?"

Lavonia shook her head. "With Katherine's illness, she is not much help in managing a household."

"I suppose taking in boarders is out of the question, then," Helen mused before biting into a biscuit.

"If Katherine were not ill so often, perhaps I could have contemplated taking in a house full of boarders. But I do not see how I could provide the comforts they would expect along with tending to Katherine when she has her spells."

"That would be burdensome, indeed." Helen sighed. "I almost wish Luke and I needed somewhere to live. Then we could buy your home."

"That is a lovely thought, but I hardly think either of you would want to exchange life in the country for a place in the city."

"True." Helen let out a sigh. "Yet, I suppose it is the right thing to do—selling the old place."

Lavonia felt a tug at her heart as she thought of never returning to the only home she had ever known. Lavonia swallowed before speaking aloud. "Selling the house is God's blessing, really."

"I remember so many good times there."

"Yes. We did have good times. Lovely times."

Both women were silent for a moment, each immersed in her own memories. The ability to share stillness in comfort was a pleasant result of their lifelong friendship.

After a few moments, Lavonia broke the quiet, "Speaking of hearth and home, Katherine and I will not be imposing on you much longer. As soon as the house is sold, I will make new arrangements for us."

"Do not hurry to leave, dear cousin! You may stay with us as long as you wish, although I fancy you will not be here long before one of our very own eligible bachelors becomes a serious suitor."

"On the contrary," Lavonia said with a chuckle. "*You* are the one who could always attract men like bees to honey."

"If you cannot see your own beauty then your mirror must be lying to you," Helen defended. "I know women who would nearly kill for such beautiful dark hair and skin as creamy as yours. I am just glad you were safely tucked away in Dover when Luke was courting me!"

Lavonia blushed. "You are too kind."

"I am not." Helen leaned toward Lavonia as if to reveal a great confidence. "A prospect has asked after you already."

"How can that be? I have only been here since Monday."

"Apparently he caught a glimpse of you upon your arrival here."

Lavonia tried to remember everyone who greeted her. "He was here, at the house?"

"Oh yes. He visits often." Helen's sly smile indicated she took pleasure in the intrigue.

"Why did he not introduce himself, then?"

"Perhaps he was too shy. Or in a hurry," she suggested. "He mentioned his infatuation with you to my dear husband on Tuesday."

"Did he say that he was infatuated with me?"

"He did not say so directly, but I could tell by the way Luke related the story." Helen's eyes were full of mischief.

"Just upon seeing me?" Lavonia took a sip of tea, savoring the feel of cool china against her lower lip. "Is this mystery man always so taken with women to whom he has not been properly introduced?"

"Hardly. He is quite upstanding. I am sure he could see your good breeding in the way you carry yourself." Leaning back in her chair, Helen looked as though she could barely contain her glee.

"You seem to enjoy matchmaking, Helen."

"I do like the promise of a new courtship," she admitted.

"You should be finding the promise of your own new marriage far more intriguing."

"I do. Which is why I want you to be happily wed, too." Helen smiled over her teacup. "So, have you no curiosity as to the identity of your admirer?"

Lavonia shrugged. "I suppose not."

"But curiosity on either side has gotten many a woman to the altar."

"Who said I want to go to the altar?"

"Is marriage not every woman's dream?" Helen asked. Not waiting for Lavonia to answer the question, Helen offered a hint. "Your prospective suitor is a man of learning."

"Is he?" Lavonia took a sip of her tea. Looking over the rim of her cup, Lavonia could see that Helen was enjoying her little game.

"And he is well respected."

"I am sure I may take you at your word."

Helen's expression turned from childlike to exasperated. "Oh, Lavonia, do you not care to venture a guess?"

"How can I guess? I know no one here."

"True." Leaning toward her, Helen gave Lavonia a pat on the hand. "You have been so patient, putting aside your own concerns to care for your sister. My sainted aunt and uncle must be looking down upon you now from heaven and thinking what a dutiful and lovely daughter you are."

Lavonia nodded to show she was grateful for Helen's kind words. The motion was all she could manage. Talking about her parents was still too difficult for her.

Helen said, her voice more chipper, "Now that your mourning time has passed, you may go to all the festivities you like."

"I am looking forward to wearing pretty colors again," Lavonia admitted. "Surely the Lord would not mind my indulgence in a bit of color after wearing black for so long." Lavonia looked at Helen's fashionable dress. The mint-green frock was set off by an emerald-colored ribbon tied in a bow just under the bodice. Yards of elegant material flowed almost to the floor, giving Helen's form a cloudy effect, as if she floated wherever she went. "That dress sets off your eyes beautifully, Helen."

Helen looked down as if relishing the fresh color. "This frock is one my dear Luke admires as well." She looked at Lavonia's face. "I have a thought! We can have a lovely gown made for you in blue to go with your eyes. Or perhaps yellow to complement your dark hair."

"Your offer is generous, Helen, but I have no designs upon becoming a social butterfly." Lavonia hesitated. She was loath to spoil her cousin's good intentions, but she wanted Helen to know about her plans. "Helen, I have a confidence I would like to share with you."

"A confidence?" Smiling, Helen placed her teacup in its saucer. Her eyes widened with anticipation. "Let me guess. You are already engaged! That is why you have been so indifferent to talk of new suitors. Tell me, who is the lucky man?" Her words rushed together.

"My situation is just the opposite. You see, I simply cannot avail myself of a courtship right away." Lavonia was well aware that her words would not be welcome to her match-making cousin. As a feeling of nervousness overcame her, Lavonia became conscious that she was squeezing a portion of uneaten biscuit, causing crumbs to fall on her dress. With a quick motion, she stuffed the treat into her mouth in a most unladylike way before sweeping the remains from her lap.

"Oh," was all Lavonia heard Helen say in response. Her cousin's voice became compassionate. "Well, that is perfectly understandable. No one here will hurry you."

"I am not afraid of being rushed. What I mean to say is, I might not avail myself of a courtship," Lavonia paused before uttering the last two words, "at all."

Helen did not bother to conceal her shock. "If you do not find a suitor, what options are left for you, Lavonia? Certainly you do not plan to become a school teacher or a governess?"

"Neither. I want to be a missionary in America."

"America! That untamed wilderness, full of savages and

who knows what other dangers? Your background hardly qualifies you for such hardship."

"If Jane Fairfield can endure the rigors of America, why should I not be able to do so?"

"Jane Fairfield? Is she your friend who married the Methodist circuit rider?"

"Yes."

"Surely you do not plan to become a Methodist, Lavonia!"

Lavonia took a sip of her tea, which had become lukewarm. "I already have, Helen. And so did Mama and Father."

In a dramatic expression of shock, Helen picked up the fan she kept nearby and began waving it in fast motions near her face. "I never thought I would hear of your family abandoning our sacred Church of England! Where is your loyalty?"

"Methodism and Anglicanism are not so different, really. Methodism's founder, John Wesley, was a lifelong Anglican."

"So you say," Helen said. "I pray worshiping with us will return you to your senses!"

"One can always pray."

Her fit of apoplexy spent, Helen placed her fan near her empty plate. "Riding over the countryside and preaching to far-flung congregations is a difficult ministry!"

"I agree." Lavonia nodded. "Jane rarely sees her husband since his circuit takes him far away from home. And he is often sick because of the inclement weather and hard conditions he must endure. But Jane is very happy, and she knows she is contributing to the Lord's work by being his wife."

"Perhaps she is a missionary, in her own way. But how do you know she is happy?" Helen's eyebrows rose in an expression of doubt.

"Her letters indicate she is quite happy."

"You must remember," Helen argued, "Jane's family had already moved to Georgia before she married. She has been accustomed to the hardships of pioneer life for many years.

And must I add, she has her own home and husband. Where would you live if you went overseas?"

"With Jane and her family, of course. She has already said she would be exhilarated to have me help her with church work. No doubt she will need me to help with household tasks. She has already borne five children and is expecting her next this winter."

"Six children? Obviously the good circuit rider makes his way home upon occasion."

Lavonia blushed. "Helen, you and Katherine are the only people in whom I have confided my plans. Except for Jane, of course. And Mama. In fact," Lavonia added, "I promised Mama on her deathbed that I would do it."

Helen's mouth dropped open in surprise. "She made you promise to be a missionary? That seems a tall order unless you are called by God to such a vocation."

"I have felt called to be a missionary for years. I was afraid to admit it. Some people would think a woman silly to undertake such a lofty vocation. Mama did not make me promise to be a missionary to fulfill her dreams for me, but for me to fulfill my own dreams. She wanted to make sure I would not take the route that you, and the rest of society, so kindly have planned for me." Lavonia could not resist letting a touch of sarcasm color her voice.

"Surely there is nothing strange about marriage."

"Of course not. Marriage is an honorable institution. I just have no reason to think marriage is the Lord's plan for me." It was Lavonia's turn to lean close to Helen. "Having to sell the house confirms my feelings about His will. The proceeds from the sale will allow both Katherine and me to be comfortable. Do you remember Aunt Amelia?"

"I remember her as disagreeable." Helen grimaced.

"But she harbors a place in her heart for Katherine. I think Katherine reminds Aunt Amelia of her daughter."

"Has it really been ten years since Elizabeth's death?"

Lavonia nodded. "Aunt Amelia has invited Katherine to come live with her. Her home is quite comfortable, really, and she employs two servants. Katherine will be well cared for, and her inheritance will go far in such a situation." Lavonia spoke faster as her excitement increased. "Once Katherine is settled, I will take my portion of the proceeds from the house to go to America! Helen, I have spent many nights praying about this. I am certain the Lord, by forcing me to part with every material possession I have in the world, is showing me the narrow path I must take to fulfill my calling. I am exchanging one life, the one of marriage, for another. The mission field."

"But I find it difficult to believe no man has even tempted you. Could you be resisting temptation on purpose, thinking you are following the Lord's will?" Helen challenged.

"If the Lord has someone for me to wed, I am sure He will swiftly inform me."

"Oh, Lavonia," Helen said softly, as if she had given up trying to argue with Lavonia. "I do envy you."

"You? Envy me?"

"Yes. You seem not to care a whit about the things of the world. I daresay you are closer to God than anyone else I have ever met."

"Helen, I wish I were the person you describe."

"I think you are. Lavonia, you are not afraid of following Him, even when it means giving up all conventions. Perhaps that is why I have always favored you."

"And I, you." Lavonia looked into Helen's eyes. "You are one of the few people left in the world I feel I can trust."

"Then let me take the liberty of giving you some counsel." She fixed her eyes on Lavonia, a deep concern on her face. "No matter how much you believe you will never marry, keep an open heart." Then Helen's tone became playful.

"After all, there are missionaries living in wedded bliss, are there not?"

They were interrupted by Helen's maid before she could respond. "Mr. Syms requests your presence in the drawing room, Madame."

"Oh! It must be our dear Dr. Amory."

"Excellent. Perhaps he's the doctor who can cure Katherine."

"If he cannot, no one practicing medicine can," Helen assured her. "Let us go and pay him our respects."

Upon arriving in the well-appointed drawing room, they found Helen's husband, Luke, waiting for them. As Lavonia had expected, in his company was a man she had never met.

"That's him!" Helen whispered, her eyes alight with prospect.

"The doctor?"

"No. Our clergyman, Osmond Gladstone." Helen checked to make certain the men were still engrossed in their own conversation. Satisfied that they had not been noticed, Helen muttered, "Lavonia, he is your secret admirer!"

two

With quick, subtle glances, Lavonia observed her admirer. Vicar Gladstone stood straight and firm, as if attempting to compensate for his short stature. His bushy hair was in need of a comb, although the action might have only served to add more white flakes to the ones already resting on the shoulders of his dark coat.

"Good morning, ladies!" Luke greeted them upon noticing their arrival. Luke introduced Lavonia to the vicar.

"How do you do, Miss Penn?" The vicar's face betrayed his interest in Lavonia.

It is true, then. The vicar may be regarding me as a prospective bride.

Although Lavonia wanted nothing more than to escape, she knew her hosts and their guest expected her to be seated for a visit. Lavonia chose a wing chair, while Helen seated herself by Lavonia on the matching sofa upholstered in gold brocaded fabric. Luke took the seat beside his wife. Then the vicar sat on the second wing chair as if it were a throne and Lavonia and the Syms were his courtiers.

"As I was saying before the ladies arrived, I am certain the bishop has great plans for me." The vicar's voice was tuned to a volume more suited to the pulpit than social discourse. Lavonia surmised he wanted to impress everyone with his confidence in the bishop's favorable assessment.

"The bishop would be a fool not to employ your learning and talents to the fullest for the Church." Lavonia wondered if Luke really believed the encouragement he offered his friend.

14

Cutting her glance to Helen, Lavonia saw her cousin smile at Luke. She wondered if he was playing Helen's matchmaking game to appease his wife.

Lavonia found herself praying silently, *If the vicar serves as my temptation from the mission field, Lord, You need not worry.*

The vicar turned his attention to Lavonia. "Will you be staying here long, Miss Penn?"

"The date of my departure is not set, Vicar."

"I trust you are having a pleasant stay with your cousin." Though he presumed to address Lavonia, the vicar gave Helen a deferential smile.

"Indeed." Hoping to signal the end of their discourse, she feigned fascination with Helen's botanical-patterned wall paper.

The vicar paused. Lavonia knew he was waiting for her to offer fodder for more queries, but she remained silent.

The vicar adjusted his spectacles and grasped for another topic. "Is the food here not delightful?"

Lavonia granted him a cursory glance with her answer. "Indeed it is."

"Everyone is always trying to steal Betsy from my employ," Helen said. "Her skill in the culinary arts is well known."

"Her reputation is deserved. I have had the pleasure of enjoying many dinners here," the vicar added, clearly wanting Lavonia to know he was a close family friend. "The menus are always agreeable. If I may be so bold as to entrust you with a confidence, Miss Penn, I must admit I do not enjoy the fare at my other parishioners' homes as well."

"Your confidence seems to be rather public," Lavonia observed. "You must not be too fearful your other parishioners will take offense lest they discover your true feelings."

"I was merely saying your cousin is kind enough to consider my palate." The vicar's even tone revealed his displeasure at her challenge. "Unfortunately, a disagreeable meal causes me to suffer *l'indignite*."

"Really? How so?"

"Too much rich food, I am afraid," he said with a chuckle.

Luke came to Osmond's rescue. "I think my dear friend means to say he suffers from *la dyspepsie*."

"Indigestion?" Though Lavonia contained a giggle, she could not resist a witty retort. "I do agree, suffering from *la dyspepsie* is indeed an indignity!"

"*Touché!*" Helen laughed. "Our Lavonia is quite the wit, is she not?"

The vicar's expression had turned sour. "Yes, she is. How clever, Miss Penn."

"Oh, do not be so glum, Osmond!" Luke chided. "If I recall, you told me only moments before the ladies arrived how much you value wit."

He smiled, though not in the way of one who was pleased. "Indeed, or as the French would say, *vraiment!*"

Luke gave the vicar a grin. "There now, you are as well-versed as Miss Penn in French after all, *oui?*"

"*Oui.* Perhaps you could lend me some of your *esprit* to add sparkle to my Sunday sermons, Miss Penn," the vicar suggested, apparently invigorated by the flattery.

"I think it most wise to leave sermonizing to men of learning, Vicar Gladstone."

"It is rare to find a woman who appreciates a man of learning." He let out an exaggerated sigh. "A man of faith often feels *l'aliènation*."

"Insane? Yes, people of faith sometimes are construed as such, though they rarely are. I entertain the notion that those who do not believe in the Lord are more likely suffering such an affliction than are people of faith."

To Lavonia's puzzlement, Vicar Gladstone's face fell. She could see his jaw muscle tense, and then he turned away from her and began talking to Luke.

Helen leaned toward Lavonia and whispered, "I think he meant to say he feels alienated, not insane."

Lavonia felt a rush of heat bring redness to her cheeks before she burst out with a gale of laughter.

Helen began laughing as well. Soon the sound of giggling filled the entire room.

Luke looked at Helen. "This is becoming a merry household indeed!"

"A bit too merry, I should observe, for a young woman in mourning attire." The vicar's look betrayed his disapproval.

"Lavonia's time of mourning is nearly over. Can you not pardon a little mirth a few days early?" Helen pleaded.

At that moment, the maid interrupted. "Pardon me, Mr. Syms. The doctor is here."

"Yes. We have been expecting him. See him to the parlor," Luke instructed.

Helen rose to exit, and the men stood as etiquette required. "Shall we accompany you, Helen, dear?"

"That shall not be necessary, my dearest Luke."

"Perhaps I should be going." Vicar Gladstone said.

"Do stay," Helen insisted. "Lavonia and I shall return momentarily. Lavonia, you do want to meet the doctor who will be treating Katherine?"

"That would be prudent, I am sure," Lavonia answered, rising from her chair. *Even the company of an uninteresting old doctor would be better than that of this pompous boor*, she thought.

Helen slowed her pace as they entered the expansive hallway. Looking back to make certain they were out of earshot of Luke and Vicar Gladstone, Helen paused in front of a portrait of herself as a young girl displayed just above a small oval-shaped mahogany table.

Following Helen's lead, Lavonia stopped.

"Well?" Helen asked, eagerness to make a match evident in her voice and expression. "What do you think of Osmond?"

Unwilling to hurt Helen's feelings by sharing the unvarnished truth, Lavonia opted for a nebulous observation. "I seem to have offended him by laughing while wearing a mourning dress. Perhaps he would have forgiven me had I been wearing my night dress instead!"

"He is not usually so sour, I assure you. He is nervous about meeting you for the first time, and no doubt feels he must play his role as vicar."

"And yet he has no more sincerity than an actor."

"I said I had a prospective suitor for you, not someone as perfect as the Lord Himself!"

Lavonia clasped Helen's hands in hers. "I truly regret I cannot envision myself as a match for the vicar, Helen. I know you have my best interests at heart."

Helen gave Lavonia's hands a gentle squeeze before releasing her grasp. "You know I do, Lavonia. And our vicar's, as well. Osmond needs someone like you. You are just the woman to mold him into the best vicar he can be. Would that not be a more agreeable missionary post than your plans to raise Jane's six children in the wilderness?"

"No," Lavonia blurted. Then, noticing Helen's look of disappointment, she added, "I would make a match with the right suitor, if I am convinced God sent him for me."

"Better for us to turn our attention to more immediate concerns," Helen said, conceding defeat for the moment as they neared the parlor. "Our doctor has been with us for some time. Katherine is certain to like him."

Lavonia nodded. She formed a mental picture of Dr. Amory: portly and bald, with a few strands of white hair combed over a shiny scalp. His expression would be like that of a father, reflecting both concern and competence. *Yes, Dr. Amory will be ideal for my sister.*

"Good morning, Dr. Amory," Helen greeted him.

The tall man standing in the parlor, his form framed by emerald-colored draperies decorating the picture window, did not fit Lavonia's image. Chiseled features were surrounded by a mass of black curls, and his posture, straight but relaxed, was a testimony to his self-assuredness.

"Good morning, Mrs. Syms." After letting his gaze rest for an instant on Helen, he glanced Lavonia's way.

Lavonia felt her own eyes widen in response. *Is he interested in me, or is it just my imagination?*

Always the hostess, Helen said, "This is Miss Lavonia Penn. Lavonia, this is Dr. William Amory."

The doctor flashed a smile that lit the room more effectively than a hundred candles could have as he answered in a sonorous voice. "*Enchant*è, Miss Penn."

At that moment, all the amusing French phrases Lavonia ever knew escaped her. Hoping her voice wouldn't quiver with excitement, she looked up into his face and uttered, "*Enchant*è!"

To Lavonia's surprise, Helen's eyebrows shot up in reprimand. "I regret Miss Penn and her sister will only be with us a short while, Dr. Amory. I hope their brief stay will nonetheless give you sufficient time to treat her sister Katherine effectively." The warmth had left her voice.

"I shall do everything in the power of God and medicine to cure my new patient." Though he was answering Helen, Dr. Amory's deep violet eyes focused on Lavonia. His soothing voice revealed confidence tempered with kindness.

Lavonia studied his features. They were strong and clean, perfect for a fine portrait.

"Have you sat for a portrait recently, Miss Penn?"

"Me? Why, Dr. Amory, I was thinking to myself that you should be the one sitting for a portrait."

"Really, Lavonia!" Obviously embarrassed by Lavonia's unexpected flirtation, Helen tried to rescue the situation. "You must excuse my cousin. She is quite devout and intent on becoming a missionary to America. Despite her impeccable lineage, she forgets the manners expected of her in civilized society."

"So you plan to be a missionary, Miss Penn?" The doctor's voice held no reproach.

Helen intervened before Lavonia could answer. "Miss Penn aspires to go to America, but she may find mission work here in England. In fact, Vicar Gladstone is in the drawing room with Luke now."

Lavonia bit her tongue to keep from disputing Helen's implications. It seemed as if Helen were deliberately trying to discourage the doctor.

Dr. Amory did not seem vexed. "In consideration of your plans, this is an excellent time for you to sit for a portrait, Miss Penn. Your family would treasure a permanent image of how you look now, just before embarking upon your life's work."

"Lavonia gives no thought to such extravagances, Doctor." Helen turned to Lavonia. "Dr. Amory studied to be an artist before pursuing medicine. He still paints the occasional portrait when he is not occupied with his chosen profession. Many women have been his muse."

"Are you not also to be my muse, Mrs. Syms?" he asked Helen.

Helen began fanning her face. "Luke asked Dr. Amory to paint a portrait of me to be hung over the mantel, a present for our first wedding anniversary."

"What a fine gesture!" Lavonia turned to the doctor. "I hope you can do her portrait justice, Dr. Amory. She is a beautiful woman."

"So, Miss Penn, will you be staying here long enough to have your portrait commissioned as well?"

"It is doubtful she will be here that long. She anticipates her move greatly," Helen responded.

Why does Helen act as though I have lost my ability to speak? Aloud Lavonia said, "By your leave, I will let my sister know you have arrived."

"A marvelous suggestion," Helen responded. "Doctor, why do we not see the others in the drawing room? You will summon us when Katherine is ready, Lavonia?"

Lavonia allowed herself one last furtive glance at the doctor. *What a handsome portrait he would make indeed!*

Not wanting to linger lest they should guess she was admiring the doctor on the sly, Lavonia rushed up the massive staircase. Upon reaching the third bedchamber on the right, Lavonia tapped on the heavy door.

"Yes?" a soft voice answered.

"It is I." Lavonia entered the sick room. In the darkness, Lavonia had difficulty making out her sister's petite form lying in a lump underneath a pile of white cotton bedding. "How are you, Kitty darling?"

Lavonia's sister turned over in the bed to face her. Her dainty face, along with narrow shoulders sheltered beneath a white nightdress, seemed to melt into the down pillows and white bedclothes. Lavonia could not imagine a more angelic sight on earth.

Katherine answered, "I am not feeling well at all."

Lavonia traveled around the bedchamber, opening the curtains to let in the light.

"Must you?" The patient pulled herself up in bed.

"Yes, I must. The doctor is here to see you, and he certainly cannot examine you in the dark." To emphasize her seriousness, Lavonia threw open a window.

"No! The air makes my head feel worse." Katherine touched a hand to her forehead.

"The odor in this room will make the doctor feel worse."

"Any reasonable doctor should be accustomed to the odor of sick rooms." She pouted and crossed her arms over her chest.

"You may regret such a cavalier attitude when you are feeling better and find yourself conversing with the doctor in society."

"When will that occur? The days I do feel well seem to be fewer and fewer. I do not want to see another doctor," she wailed. "I must have seen every doctor in England. None of them can help me."

"You have not seen Dr. Amory." Lavonia sat on the bed beside her sister. "Is it too uncomfortable for you to sit upright, Kitty?"

"I would rather lie down, but I will sit up for you, Vonnie."

Lavonia smiled. No one else but her sister called her by that pet name. Likewise, only Lavonia called Katherine "Kitty." The name seemed to fit her sister—vulnerable, needing care and shelter from the world.

"Where does it hurt?"

"Everywhere. The side of my head, my nose, my teeth, my neck, everywhere. There is a little man inside my skull beating it with a hammer. He never stops."

Despite her sister's fanciful description, Lavonia knew she suffered. "Maybe there is something this doctor can do for you that the others could not."

Katherine took Lavonia's hand. "Please do not let him bleed me."

Lavonia could sympathize with not wanting to be sucked by leeches. She wondered how the worms knew to suck out bad blood and leave good blood for the patient to recover, and yet she said, "I am not sure how I can stop him if he thinks that is best. Who are we to question a medical doctor?"

"Vonnie, if anyone can challenge a doctor, you can. I am begging you not to let him. It only makes me feel worse." The plea in her eyes was more than Lavonia could bear.

"All right. I will see what I can do." She searched her mind for something—anything—that might help her sister. Her effort was rewarded when she recalled a letter that had arrived in the morning mail. "By the way, we received a letter from Aunt Amelia this morning."

"Auntie Amelia!" Katherine's face beamed. "How are things in London?"

"As always, she is entertaining guests and being entertained."

Katherine sighed. "How glamorous to be part of London society!"

Lavonia was not so certain, but she decided not to debate the point. "You can read all about it as soon as the doctor leaves. There, does the prospect give you something pleasant to anticipate?"

"Oh yes! You can always cheer me, Vonnie."

Pleased, Lavonia was preparing to leave as her sister's voice halted her.

"Vonnie?"

"Yes?"

"Have you met the doctor yet?"

Lavonia swallowed. "Yes."

"Do you think he is nice?"

"Yes, I do." She rose from the side of the bed before Katherine could ask her any more questions. "Let us try to assure his good temper by not keeping him waiting any longer. I am sure he has more patients he must see today." As she opened the door, Lavonia turned to take one last look at her sister. Only a mass of dark tangled curls marred her beauty. "Could you brush your hair, Kitty?"

"I was hoping you could brush it for me tonight."

Lavonia handed Katherine her brush. "I will. But try to smooth it just a little, for now?"

Seeing a nod of acquiescence, Lavonia retreated. Helen and the doctor were already in the hallway.

"I was just coming down the stairs."

"Our timing could not be better, then." Helen turned to the

doctor. "Miss Penn and I have been friends as well as family for so many years, our thoughts are as one."

"I see." His serious expression belied his light tone of voice.

A quick glance at Helen revealed that Helen was smiling at the doctor as if conveying a hidden message. *I wonder what she is really saying to him?*

"Since I am a matron, allow me to go in with the doctor," Helen told Lavonia. Although Lavonia wanted to hear what the doctor had to say for herself, she knew better than to argue. "If you are lucky, the vicar will still be with Luke."

Lavonia's lips curled. "A good reason not to believe in luck."

Lavonia wished she could retreat to her own bedchamber to avoid bantering with the vicar again, but at Helen's urgings, Lavonia did remember her manners. As predicted, he was waiting in the drawing room.

"Your parishioners must be quite well taken care of if you give them all such attentiveness," Lavonia couldn't help but comment.

The vicar let out a nervous titter. "As a matter of fact, I was just planning to leave."

"Nonsense, Osmond," Luke intervened. "We were just about to partake of our noon meal. Will you not stay with us?"

The vicar made a show of consulting his pocket watch. "Is it noon already? I did not intend to linger so long."

Luke addressed his guest in a deferential manner. "If it is an inconvenience for you to stay—"

"Oh, it is no inconvenience, at least not on my part."

"Very well. An extra place will be set for you." Luke gave Lavonia a conspiratorial smile.

"Perhaps hospitality should be extended to the doctor, as well?" Lavonia offered.

Luke looked taken aback by Lavonia's suggestion, but soon recovered. "Certainly we should accommodate all of our guests. The doctor may see fit to disappoint us, though. His practice keeps him busy."

"Yes," the vicar agreed. "The doctor seems to work day and night."

"All the more reason he should stay to eat." Lavonia smiled. "The doctor may as well accustom himself to the food here. He will be here often once he begins Helen's portrait."

"He is painting her portrait?" the vicar asked Luke.

"Oh yes. In fact, he is scheduled to begin next month."

"How does the doctor find time to paint and practice medicine as well?"

"I am not sure what you mean."

Lavonia was pleased to see Luke discern the vicar's sly tone of voice. "Yes, what do you mean to say, vicar?"

Apparently flustered, he pushed his spectacles up on his nose. "I was not aware you were planning to have Mrs. Syms' portrait painted."

"I thought she would enjoy having her portrait painted, but I did not speculate those plans would interest you, Osmond."

"But they do. Perhaps you would consider commissioning my cousin Lloyd Maxwell, instead. He has studied art and is quite talented. He is just beginning to establish himself and is having difficulty making a living with his artwork. He has no medical training to fall back on, unlike Dr. Amory." The vicar lowered his voice. "Though he would be embarrassed at my saying so, Lloyd could use the money."

"Very well. By Dr. Amory's leave, I will commission your cousin."

"I assure you, my cousin's personal reputation is impeccable."

Lavonia wondered why the vicar's voice was laden with strong overtones of intrigue. *It is almost as if he doesn't trust the good doctor. What is it about Dr. Amory that no one will discuss? Perhaps the noon meal will prove a good time to unravel the mystery.*

three

Lavonia placed a pink rose in the crystal bud vase on Katherine's luncheon tray. A whiff of soft fragrance brought a smile to her face. "The gardens are so beautiful this year, Betsy."

"That they are, Miss Penn." The stout cook lifted the top of a large cast iron pot simmering over the fire. After inspecting its contents, she whisked a large wooden spoon through them twice before returning the lid to its position. " 'Tis a pity Miss Katherine can't be outside to enjoy 'em." She gazed out of the window, a look of longing on her sweaty face. "I wonder how she endures it, closed up in that dark room as she is."

"Miss Katherine considers the darkness a blessing rather than a curse."

"Poor Miss Katherine." Betsy eyed the tray. "Would you have me call Lucy to take the tray up?"

Lavonia picked up the tray. Discovering it wasn't heavy, she shook her head. "No, thank you, Betsy. I can manage."

The older woman cast Lavonia a look filled with doubt. Nevertheless, she acquiesced with a gentle, "Yes, mum."

Lavonia's heart skipped a beat when she heard the doctor's melodic voice from Katherine's room. She paused for a second, readying herself to enter. Helen was certain to scold her for bringing the meal while the doctor was still with his new patient, but Lavonia didn't care. "I just have to know what he thinks of her condition," Lavonia appeased her conscience. She didn't want to admit, even to herself, that she might have other motives.

"I have your tray, Kitty." Lavonia kept her voice cheerful

as she entered the sick room.

"Could it not have waited until Dr. Amory left?" Helen asked.

"That is quite all right, Mrs. Syms. My visit with Miss Penn is complete." Dr. Amory gave Lavonia a look of kindness.

"Is it time for luncheon already? What did you bring?" Katherine asked.

"Roasted leg of mutton, new white potatoes, and green beans fresh from the garden." Lavonia smiled.

"Sounds delicious!" Dr. Amory said to Katherine.

Giving Lavonia a brief nod, he moved to his right to allow Lavonia access to the side of the bed. As he shifted his position, Lavonia inhaled the masculine scent of his skin, sweetened with a spicy bay rum. She wished she could linger near him, enjoying his luscious aroma. Yet Helen's disapproving stare, visible even from her position at the foot of the bed, impeded Lavonia from such indulgence.

Trying to keep her voice casual, Lavonia noted, "It is well you should think the meal delicious, Dr. Amory. If I am not mistaken, our host has made plans to extend you an invitation to dine with us." Fearing what Helen might think of the offer, Lavonia held her gaze to the doctor's face rather than seeking her cousin's affirmation.

"You can have my portion, then," Katherine said, grimacing as she surveyed her plate. "I fear I cannot stomach anything so heavy as mutton."

Lavonia set the tray on her sister's lap. "I know it is hard for you to eat when you suffer so. But perhaps something here will tempt you. Will you not try to eat something, Kitty dear?"

"For you, I might try, Vonnie."

"Pet names from childhood?" Dr. Amory asked.

"Yes. And no one else calls us that. Is that not right, Vonnie?" Katherine asked in a pointed tone.

Dr. Amory raised his eyebrows. "It is good to see two sisters so close when many of my patients bicker among their families. I wonder if too much vigorous debate contributes to a plethora of maladies."

"Dr. Amory has some interesting theories," Helen remarked.

"Helen has been telling me how brilliant you are, Dr. Amory," Lavonia said. "She has me convinced you are the only doctor alive who can cure Katherine."

"I surmise Miss Penn would not care to be cured by a doctor who is dead," quipped the lively Dr. Amory.

"Please take this food away—the smell of it turns my stomach," Katherine answered, not bothering to conceal her irritability.

"You will have to excuse my sister. Her headaches leave her in a poor temper." Lavonia turned to Katherine. "You must eat something to keep up your strength. Let us go now."

"I will eat more if you stay with me," Katherine coaxed.

"Perhaps that is a good idea," Helen said.

"Miss Penn is not suffering from malnutrition. She need not eat more than is agreeable," the doctor said. "If you do not wish to eat alone, Miss Penn, I recommend you join the party downstairs."

Katherine's eyes narrowed. "No, thank you. I am quite comfortable here."

"Very well." The doctor motioned Lavonia and Helen to join him as he exited.

"You will not stay with me, Vonnie?" Katherine pleaded.

Unable to resist her soulful cry, Lavonia glanced upon the doctor with a wordless entreaty. Instead, the lips that had seemed so full moments before straightened into a firm line as he gave her a curt shake of the head.

"I must go, Kitty," Lavonia answered. "I shall return soon." Ignoring Kitty's pout, Lavonia closed the door behind her. The doctor had already begun his brisk walk toward the staircase.

Lavonia strode to match his pace. "Why did you force me to be so cruel to her?"

As his lips tightened into an even more defiant line, Helen answered, "The doctor knows best, Lavonia."

Dr. Amory's eyes inclined toward Helen as if to express his gratitude in her confidence.

Frustrated, Lavonia pursued her inquiries as soon as they reached the bottom of the steps. "There was no reason for me to be unkind, Doctor." Lavonia felt her face flush with anger.

"Your sister says she has suffered headaches most of her life," the doctor stated.

Lavonia nodded. "They worsened when Father first became ill. Ever since Mama's death, they have kept her nearly bedridden."

His eyes focused on the massive double doors leading to the foyer. A soft sunbeam entering from the window illuminated his face. Lavonia marveled upon his smooth yet robust skin. Seeming not to notice Lavonia's admiration, he mused, "I wonder how your sister feels about your plans to go to America."

Helen intervened. "I should think Katherine would be happy for Lavonia to live out her dreams."

With a sharp motion, he turned to Helen. "Undoubtedly. Mrs. Syms, would you be so kind as to see that Miss Penn has a fresh pitcher of water in her room? It seemed a bit low, I observed."

"Indeed? But I just—"

"Please, Mrs. Syms."

Helen shot them a withering look before leaving on her directed errand. Dr. Amory motioned Lavonia to the parlor. Sensing the discussion would be brief, Lavonia did not seat herself on either mahogany chair occupying the room.

"About your plans, Miss Penn, how much does your sister know?"

"Why, everything, of course."

"And she does not mind you leaving her for America?"

"We have expressed how much we will miss each other, but she has given me no indication she does not want me to go."

The doctor looked doubtful. "Has she not? She seems quite possessive of you."

"Possessive? I have never noticed such."

"You are so close to her. I am not surprised you are not able to see her clearly."

Lavonia's eyes narrowed at the impact of his words. "Are you suggesting Katherine is pretending to have headaches to keep me here?"

"Surely she must rue the day you will depart. I suspect she has no one else to care for her when she is ill," he said. "Or at least, no one else would be nearly as attentive to her."

Lavonia's mouth tightened with anger. "I am disappointed in you, Dr. Amory. I was led to believe you are not a charlatan!"

"A charlatan?"

"Several doctors have told us headaches are an imaginary ailment of rich women who simply want to retire to their bedchambers. I assure you, Dr. Amory, contrary to what the medical profession thinks, women do not pretend to have headaches!" Lavonia's heart was thumping with fury.

"I beg your pardon, Miss Penn. It was not my intention to incite you. Despite what you think, I agree with your assessment of the medical profession's opinion." His rational demeanor contrasted wildly with her fury.

"So you say," she hissed.

"I surmise Miss Penn's other doctors feel as helpless to heal her as I do. Is it not easier to dismiss a charge when the situation seems hopeless?"

Lavonia let out a weary sigh. "Then even you think it is hopeless."

"Perhaps not entirely, at least not in your sister's case.

Unlike some of the other doctors you have visited, I do not think she feigns headaches. In an odd way, she may actually welcome the pain."

Lavonia did not bother to conceal her disgust. "That is absurd. If that is your best diagnosis, then I should never have agreed to let Katherine see you."

"My theory is not so preposterous when you consider how much attention you give her when she is ill."

"Of course I give her attention when she is ill. It is not her fault she cannot function when she is sick." Lavonia tilted her chin defiantly.

"You know your sister better than I. Perhaps she is trying to foster a sense of responsibility to keep you tied to her."

"Dr. Amory, I assure you, my sister is not manipulating me!"

He arched one eyebrow. "Then perhaps, I should say, *Ce que je lui reproche, c'est sa paresse.*"

Lavonia reflexively rose to her sister's defense. "I beg your pardon! My sister is not lazy!"

"So she has accomplished much today while lying in bed?"

Lavonia's inability to dispute his point only fueled her anger. "Dr. Amory, Katherine and I have been reviled by our share of doctors, but I have never been offended so blatantly! Accusing my sister of ulterior motives, indeed! And to think only a few moments ago, I thought you rather dashing!" Lifting her skirt ever so slightly with a quick motion to emphasize her rage, Lavonia turned to exit. Before she reached the doorway, the doctor's voice stopped her.

"If you do intend to work on the mission field, Miss Penn, I recommend you review the Scriptures on control of the tongue."

Turning her head in his direction, she saw a look of amusement on his countenance that made her huff with exasperation. "I assure you, Dr. Amory, I *am* controlling my tongue! Good day!"

Lavonia's heels clacked on the wood floor as she rapidly made her way to the dining room. *How could the doctor insult my sister and then me as well? I wish I had never suggested he be included in the luncheon. I suppose it is too much to hope he will have the good manners to decline!*

To Lavonia's regret, Dr. Amory appeared at the table. Helen had already arranged Lavonia to be seated beside him and across from Vicar Gladstone. "I wish Katherine felt better," Helen whispered to Lavonia. "Without her, the number of settings at my table is uneven."

"Perhaps she will feel better tomorrow."

"What good is tomorrow? I doubt the vicar and the doctor will be dining with us then."

They were interrupted by the vicar. "Will you allow me to lead all of us in prayer before we commence our meal?"

"I was just about to beg the favor," Luke answered.

Pushing his chair back, Osmond stood and cleared his throat. When he spoke, his voice rang throughout the house. "Our dear Father in heaven, I thank You that we who are privileged to dine at this fine table are blessed with peerless cuisine and the exalted company of the most upstanding people in our noble society. We are supremely grateful that in Your indisputable wisdom, You see fit to bless Your most upstanding servants with all of life's ephemeral pleasures. Should any among us suffer some untoward blemish, we thank You for the opportunity to dine among them, the sinners, following the example of our Lord Jesus Christ. Amen."

Surveying the party at the table, the vicar gave each one a satisfied look before returning to his seat.

"It is not often I have the opportunity to hear one pray in the true spirit of the Pharisees," Dr. Amory whispered to Lavonia.

Lavonia's lips curled at his levity in spite of her best efforts to stay mad at the doctor. "I think Vicar Gladstone is unlike most of the clergy."

"Let us hope so."

Oblivious to their remarks, Luke said, "Thank you, Osmond. Such prayers are certain to assure your place in London."

"You are seeking a London parish?" Dr. Amory asked.

"Such matters were not intended for public consumption, but certainly I can trust you to keep the confidence, Dr. Amory." Though his words conveyed conviction, the vicar's tone of voice betrayed that he wasn't sure he trusted the doctor.

"I beg your pardon, Osmond," Luke apologized. "I did not mean to violate a confidence."

The vicar waved his hand dismissively as he went on. "Since I have had the honor of serving this parish for two years, I feel the time has arrived for me to seek a larger church. London should serve my purposes quite well."

"Speaking of London, did you know we have relations there?" Helen asked. "In fact, we received a letter from our dear Aunt Amelia only today."

"How lovely. I trust she is doing well?"

Helen nodded to Lavonia. "Would you wish to share Aunt Amelia's letter with us, Lavonia?"

Lavonia acquiesced and withdrew the letter from her pocket. As always, her aunt's correspondence was written upon heavy linen paper, the color of ivory. Lavish handwriting, dotted with curly strokes and bold flourishes, conveyed her message in black india ink.

My dear nieces:

How lovely is this year's social season! I have already attended two prestigious events, and the season is still young. The first was a ball held to announce the Thorndike/Upton engagement. This marriage will unite two of London's premiere families. The Thorndikes own several properties and have made their fortune conducting business of some sort in India. And of course, the Uptons

*have connections to royalty. So as you can surmise, their
wedding is certain to be the social event of next season.*

*And that is only the beginning! Last Saturday night, a
cotillion was held at the Marshall residence. There were
over two hundred people in attendance, although naturally, only people of wealth and stature were invited to
this event. You should have been there to hear the fifty-
piece orchestra. They played encores until dawn. And
what a fabulous banquet! Space does not permit me to
list every foodstuff available there, but I did most enjoy
the roasted pheasant, lobster bisque, and oyster soup.
And so many varieties of cakes and pastries! I fear I
might have overindulged, but what is life if not to enjoy?*

*Indeed, I would love nothing more than to host my
own gala in the near future. I keep telling myself that I
should gather the servants, set a date, and plan a good
menu. But I never seem to do so. Of course, you might
ask, "Why can you not sit back and let the servants do
all the work, Aunt? After all, do you not deserve to rest
at your advanced age?" But deserving or not, I am
aware of the folly of entrusting a social event of such
magnitude to the servants when expectations run high. I
dare not disappoint! So I procrastinate.*

*But what sport is procrastination! We are enjoying a
Shakespearean revival here. I do believe I have seen
most of his plays within the past year, even those of the
more obscure variety. I hold tickets for the Wednesday
evening performance of "Hamlet" and am eager to
attend the performance with the Snidewells. Naturally,
I need not tell even you who the Snidewells are.*

*Afternoons with the Snidewells on their country estate
are met with great anticipation. Certainly your father
has mentioned the Snidewells. They made their fortune
in horse breeding. A Snidewell horse is the most desirable*

*in London society. Invitations to their intimate affairs
are extended only to their dearest friends, which of
course, includes myself. Though I sometimes become a
bit tired, I am loathe to disappoint so I make certain to
appear when summoned.*

*The servant has rung the bell for afternoon tea, so I
shall close.*

As Always,
Aunt Amelia

Folding the letter, Lavonia restrained herself from commenting upon its blatant boasting and that it never asked
after its recipients.

The vicar didn't seem to notice any breach of etiquette.
"Your aunt is acquainted with so many upstanding families.
What a fine person she must be, indeed!"

"We believe so, though we may be a bit partial," Helen
answered.

"Her letter suggests she may already be acquainted with
my future parishioners. Perhaps I might call upon her during
my next visit to London?" The vicar seemed to salivate at the
prospect.

"I am certain she would be honored to be visited by our
vicar," Luke said before casting his gaze to Lavonia. *"Oui?"*

Lavonia wasn't sure how her aunt would react to a visit
from the vicar despite their shared worldliness. "Her letters
always indicate she keeps a full calendar. She may be difficult
to reach at home."

The vicar's mouth turned down into a sour expression, but
to Lavonia's relief, he didn't press the point. Instead, he
turned to Luke and began talking. "I've done quite a job, if I
do say so myself, here in Dover. My parishioners seem well
pleased with my sermons."

As the vicar's conversation faded from her attention,

Lavonia cut her glance to the doctor. Since he seemed engrossed in the others' discourse at the far end of the table, she
allowed her stare to linger upon him. A straight nose and chiseled chin gave him a sharp and distinguished profile. She soon
forgot her anger with him and found herself fantasizing what
her days would be like if she could look upon such a comely
face forever.

For a moment their eyes met. "The vicar makes a good
point. Do you agree?"

Caught off guard, Lavonia nodded and changed the subject. "I must say, Dr. Amory, based on just a brief acquaintance, I already admire your versatility in so many subjects.
Medicine, the arts, Scripture. Where do you find time for so
many endeavors?"

His eyebrows raised. "I find time for any *worthy* endeavor,
Miss Penn." His voice had a soft quality about it, as though
he were trying to communicate something more to Lavonia.
Deliberate attempts to remember why she was angry with
him failed to reignite her wrath. Instead, his soothing tone
made her heart race for quite different reasons.

"Do you now, Doctor?" the vicar interrupted, apparently
having eavesdropped upon their conversation. "In that regard,
you may find yourself with time for yet another undertaking,
now that Mrs. Syms will be having her portrait painted by an
artist other than yourself." The vicar gave Dr. Amory a sly
smile, clearly enjoying his moment of triumph.

If Dr. Amory was taken aback, he hid his emotions well.
"Is this true, Mr. Syms? You no longer wish me to paint your
wife's portrait?"

"As a matter of fact—"

"Why, of course he does!" Helen looked at her husband at
the opposite end of the table. "Luke, you have not changed
your mind about having my portrait painted, have you? I was
so looking forward to it."

"I have decided to commission Osmond's cousin."

The vicar's mouth curled into a victorious grin.

Luke continued, "He is a practicing artist and is highly recommended."

"By the vicar, no doubt," Helen observed.

"Naturally, I should recommend my cousin. But only because he possesses a large degree of talent," the vicar hastened to add.

"Oh, I see," Dr. Amory said.

Luke gave him a sympathetic look. "I beg your forgiveness, Doctor. Apparently our vicar did not know I had not yet spoken to you about my change in plans." His tight-lipped delivery belied the defense of his friend.

"Nor did you inform me," Helen said.

"Had I known Osmond had a cousin who paints portraits, I would not have burdened our doctor with such work when he undoubtedly has many patients in need of his healing powers. But I only learned of the vicar's cousin this very day." As if verbalizing the breach caused Luke to realize his error, he added, "Of course, I will pay you a percentage of the commission you would have earned had you completed the picture, Dr. Amory."

"That is quite all right," said the doctor. "I am not so destitute that I need take money for nothing."

"But I insist."

"As do I, Dr. Amory," Helen added, clearly vexed. "The vicar is a childhood friend of my husband's, which is why loyalty has taken precedence over his manners regarding your engagement. I implore you to accept the compensation he offers in return for your inconvenience."

"Regarding manners," Luke said, "where are ours, to discuss business over such a delightful lunch? And, my dear Helen, why are you worrying your beautiful head over business? That is a man's job, *oui?*"

"*Oui.*" Helen gave him a smile that showed she was ready to drop the subject and return to lighter topics.

"How easily they forgive each other," the doctor whispered to Lavonia.

"The effects of newly wedded bliss, no doubt." Resolute in her intention not to show him his effect on her, she added, "One that you and I do not enjoy."

"I beg your pardon for offending you earlier. Truly, that was not my intent." Features softening, his eyes shone with regret.

Lavonia tried to keep her voice curt. "What was your intent, then?"

"To free you both."

Surprised by such an answer, Lavonia didn't answer right away, then she whispered, "Free us?"

"That is correct."

"Who said I want to be free of my own sister?"

"It is obvious that you will either go to the mission field or become betrothed to Vicar Gladstone and care for your sister here, if Mrs. Syms has her way."

"Perish the thought."

The doctor chuckled quietly. The others at the table were engrossed in their own conversation. "Have you told Mrs. Syms yet?"

Lavonia swallowed a piece of mutton. "She knows my first priority is going to America. I have no time for suitors."

"I am certain that preparing for your journey is a time-consuming endeavor. You are blessed to have a house to sell, so that the proceeds may secure your passage."

Lavonia gently patted her lips with her napkin. "How did you become privy to such information?"

"Mrs. Syms mentioned a few of the circumstances surrounding your visit when she first spoke to me about your sister. She did not indicate to me she was telling me in confidence," he apologized as he speared a few green beans with his silver fork.

"Well, I think it is God's will for the house to be sold. He is making the way for me to go to the mission field."

"Your faith makes me wonder."

"Wonder what?"

"If God is telling me that I, too, must alter my plans due to a change in circumstance. You see, my benefactor recently passed away."

"I am sorry to hear that. Was he a close relation?"

"Not at all. In fact, I only knew his name. Philemon Midas. Does that name sound familiar to you?"

Lavonia took a sip of tea. "Of course, Midas was a mythological figure. And the New Testament book of Philemon is an epistle of Saint Paul."

"Yes. Written to a wealthy man named Philemon. But you know no one by that name?"

"No. Why should I?"

"It has been my impression Mr. Midas was from somewhere near Dover."

"I suppose it is possible. I am not familiar with everyone in the area." Lavonia finished the last of her green beans. "Whomever he is, I wonder why he chose to be your benefactor, since you obviously didn't know him if you didn't even know where he lived. So what are these plans of yours?"

Before he could answer, they were interrupted by Lucy the maid. "Mr. Joseph Penn is here."

"Mr. Penn? An excellent surprise indeed!" said Luke. "Do see him in."

"I wonder why Uncle Joseph is here now. I was not expecting him until next week," Lavonia wondered aloud.

"I did not realize Joseph Penn is your uncle." Dr. Amory was clearly surprised.

"Yes." Lavonia noticed the doctor's rich complexion had turned the color of Helen's bone china. "Why? Is anything the matter, doctor?"

"Good day to all of you!" Uncle Joseph's voice boomed as

he entered the dining room. "How fortuitous for me to time my arrival for lunch!" His glance stopped short when he spied the doctor. Suddenly, Uncle Joseph's jovial tone turned taut.

"William Amory. What are you doing here?"

four

Dr. Amory rose to greet Lavonia's uncle, though he did not offer his hand. "Good day to you as well."

The irony in the doctor's salutation did not escape Lavonia.

Uncle Joseph glared at Dr. Amory as if his presence violated all forms of decency. "I was not aware of your friendship with the Syms family. And I certainly had no indication you are acquainted with my niece."

If the doctor was disturbed by the suspicion in Uncle Joseph's tone of voice, his blank expression didn't betray him as he sat back down. "I have been the Syms' family doctor for some time now. However, I have had the pleasure of meeting your nieces only today."

"Katherine is Dr. Amory's newest patient," Helen explained.

Uncle Joseph didn't conceal his surprise. "Katherine is ill?"

Dr. Amory's eyebrow crooked. "You are unaware your younger niece suffers with chronic headaches?"

"No, I was not aware of her malady," Uncle Joseph muttered, his sharp features becoming sanguine with embarrassment. "Naturally, I am pleased she is seeking a cure. I do hope her treatment proves successful." ·

As if he really cares, Lavonia thought. Aloud she said, "We have had very little contact with Uncle Joseph until recently. He is handling Mama's estate, so he is apprised primarily of our financial, not our personal, affairs."

Rising from his seat at the head of the table, Luke interrupted. "Let us not spoil luncheon by discussion of finances. Will you not dine with us, Mr. Penn? Surely business is conducted more pleasantly when one's appetite is satiated."

41

Lavonia noticed Dr. Amory's body stiffen. He took a bite of mutton, chewing it with deliberate concentration as if in an effort to remain silent.

"I am not here on a social call, but on a matter of business with my niece," Uncle Joseph protested in a manner most unconvincing. "I regret my visit here shall be brief and will allow me little time for pleasantries."

Lavonia placed her white linen napkin beside the delicate bone china luncheon plate. "Perhaps we should excuse ourselves so we might proceed with our business, Uncle?"

Ignoring Lavonia, Uncle Joseph's gaze roved over the generous portion of leg of mutton situated on the platter in the center of the ample dining room table. "Though, I might make room for a bite of lunch."

The shifting of chairs, plates, and accouterments followed as he sat down to the meal. Considering his substantial girth, Lavonia was not surprised to witness her uncle consuming large portions of meat and the remaining bread, though he seemed to have a noticeable aversion to green beans.

As the vicar began citing his own accomplishments, Lavonia's mind tried to guess the purpose of her uncle's unannounced visit. The house had been for sale almost a year. Perhaps a buyer had been found. She prayed that if that were so, the price offered was enough to secure a comfortable future for both Katherine and herself.

Preoccupied, Lavonia remained quiet for the rest of the meal. A glance Dr. Amory's way near the completion of the plum pudding revealed a sullen expression on his face; his spirits had been dampened as well.

Dr. Amory was fine before my uncle arrived. Obviously they know each other. I wonder in what context? And what soured their relationship?

Lavonia had no time to inquire after the meal since both the doctor and vicar departed minutes after dessert. Unable to postpone the encounter any longer, Lavonia nervously followed her uncle into the parlor. She stood in front of the picture window as she watched her uncle plop himself upon the cushioned sofa and give his stomach a satisfied pat. Ignoring his tasteless gesture, she said, "I surmise your visit must be about the affairs of Mama's estate. Otherwise, I cannot fathom why you would journey all this way."

"Yes, it is. I regret this matter has taken so much time to resolve. As you are aware, the courts in London are chronically backlogged. And the fact that your mother had inherited a small parcel of land in another jurisdiction complicates matters all the more." Slowly he bent his arm over the side of the sofa and picked up the brown leather portfolio resting on the floor. Pulling it onto his lap, he opened it and withdrew several papers.

Lavonia's stomach lurched with nervous anticipation and a flood of hope that the documents contained good news. "Are those to clear the sale of the land?"

"No, these are another matter entirely." He handed Lavonia the papers. "I thought it best to see if you could explain them, though certainly such business is well beyond the feeble intellect of your gender."

At his barb, her anticipation transformed into animosity. Hiding her feelings, Lavonia calmly took the papers from his outstretched hand. Then taking a seat on a hard mahogany bench, she examined several letters demanding payment on overdue bills. As she read, her ire grew.

These should have been paid months ago!

Revealing his impatience at her delay in commenting, her uncle interrupted her thoughts. "Those are letters from your many creditors. They demand prompt payment," he explained as if she were an obtuse child.

"I can see that." She gave him a level stare. "So why have they not been paid?"

"Simply because I refuse to pay bills far beyond what should have constituted your normal household expenses. I fail to understand why the merchants in question insist your father made these purchases." He paused. "Look at the bill from Dover Fire and Fuel." As Lavonia rifled through the bills, he continued, "They say your family purchased ten tons of coal in January 1813. I hardly believe you could have burned that much fuel."

Lavonia read the bill. "Your assessment is correct. Ten tons is double the amount we generally consume over an entire year."

Uncle Joseph raised his bushy black eyebrows. "I see you possess some knowledge of household finances. Then you can dispute these claims."

"I will not dispute them, because Father did indeed make these purchases." Tilting her chin upward, she returned the stack of bills to her uncle.

His mouth opened in a show of shock. "Are you trying to say your father spent over a thousand pounds in fuel, food, and clothing last year?" The pitch of his voice rose with apparent disbelief. He stood and paced the rug as if his apoplectic fit would be relieved by the exercise. "Preposterous! That is more than he should have spent in three years! The merchants are attempting to take advantage!"

"No, they are not," Lavonia protested. "If you had been in touch with us at all these past decades, you would know the reason for these obligations. You see, Uncle Joseph, my father was not only generous with Mama and me, but with the less fortunate as well. Thanks to his largesse, many people were fed, clothed, and kept warm each winter."

Stopping in his tracks, Uncle Joseph turned to face Lavonia. His already pale complexion had become several shades whiter. "Is that so? And how did he manage to form such attachments with the lower classes?"

"My father felt the Lord's calling to use a large portion of his wealth to help the poor, whether they had been poverty-stricken their entire lives, or members of the upper classes who were experiencing temporary difficulties."

He shivered visibly. "And he allowed his daughter to mingle with these people?"

"I would have considered it an honor to meet those he helped." Lavonia bristled.

Uncle Joseph raised his eyebrows. "You never met any of them?"

She shook her head. "No one but Father was acquainted with the details of his ministry. He sought no publicity or fame."

"Fool," he muttered.

Lavonia was certain she wasn't meant to overhear her uncle's unbridled opinion. "Dear Father was a kind and generous man," she countered nevertheless.

Her uncle sniffed. "What you consider kind, others would think eccentric."

"I have no qualms about paying for Father's *largesse*." Emphasizing the last word, Lavonia squared her shoulders. "Please inform my creditors that the bills will be paid in full as soon as the house is sold."

"Oh yes." He lifted his forefinger. "The house. That is another matter."

"You have news, then?"

"Yes, and I am afraid it is not good. Your home did not fetch the price I expected. Indeed, the proceeds from it are thousands of pounds lower than anticipated."

"Thousands of pounds? That is preposterous. The price I asked is more than fair." Lavonia lifted her chin. "I will simply not accept the offer."

Uncle Joseph shook his head. "That is not possible. The papers have been signed, and the sale is complete."

"Complete? How can that be? I have not signed, nor even seen, any deed of sale."

"The original deeds are in my London office. I have left a duplicate set of papers with Luke for safekeeping."

Realizing she was helpless to reverse the transaction, Lavonia's heart beat with fear. Her mouth became too dry for her to speak.

However, her uncle was not deterred. "It has also come to my attention that thousands of pounds have disappeared with no record of their whereabouts. Can you explain that?"

Lavonia was shocked. She cast about, trying to come up with a reason for the money to be missing. But the situation was too much to comprehend. Her head bowing, she felt her shoulders, moments ago set in pride, droop with anguish. "No."

"I thought not." Her uncle sniffed. "Are you aware that I have been paying Luke for your living expenses plus your allowance while the will went through probate?"

She nodded.

"Those expenses are not inconsequential. Consider yourself fortunate to have an uncle wise in the ways of business. Unlike your father, I have preserved my share of the family fortune. Indeed, it has increased fourfold under my stewardship."

"So you have informed me in previous conversations."

"Had your problems resulted merely from my brother's spendthrift ways, they might not be so severe. But as you remember, your mother was consumed with wasteful spending as well." Stretching the fingers of his left hand, he ticked off a list with the forefinger of his right hand. "Trips abroad. Fine clothing. Furnishings imported from America."

"We had a lovely home and many opportunities," Lavonia argued in her mother's defense.

"I hope you enjoyed that home and those opportunities of the past. Because of their expense, your future might not be so pleasing."

Pictures of happy times flashed through her mind. Setting her jaw as she gazed at him, she kept her voice strong. "I have no regrets."

"So you say." He paused. "But those times are past, and now you must face the future. How do you think you shall do that?"

Unable to answer, Lavonia swallowed.

His voice brightened. "There is a solution to your dilemma."

She looked into his eyes. "Yes?"

"Marriage."

"Marriage?"

"Of course." He looked down his nose. "Surely you have contemplated marriage."

"I have not."

"Then you would do well to reconsider."

I dare not tell Uncle Joseph betrothal is not in my plans. How can it be, when I promised Mama I would be a missionary? Or perhaps I should tell him, so he will know how important it is for me to secure money for my trip to America. Rising from her seat, Lavonia opened her lips to speak but his firm expression made her change her mind. *No, I cannot say anything. Anyone who looks down on Father's compassion would never understand our faith.*

Uncle Joseph's eyes roved over her from the top of her deep-brown hair to the hem of her black mourning dress. "Perhaps a rich man can overlook poverty in exchange for a good family name and a pretty face."

Lavonia shivered at his lascivious attention. "I have no desire for a husband, and I would certainly never marry for worldly gain."

"I assure you, the realities of pauperism will alter your perspective." The smile her uncle gave Lavonia was unpleasant, as if he looked forward to watching her suffer.

Lavonia stiffened. "I am prepared to live in poverty."

He let out a small huff. "Romantic notions aside, you must reconcile your family's debts. It makes me sick to think how my brother was taken advantage of." Uncle Joseph sneered. "The slothful and ne'er-do-wells of this world can spot rich eccentrics from miles away. They are skilled at playing upon their sympathies. Where are the beggars now? Look around, Lavonia," he said, sweeping his hand over the room. "Do you see any of them here to help you?"

"The Bible says not to invite rich people to dinner because they can repay you. Instead, invite the poor, who cannot repay."

"Is that what it says? Poor advice for one who plans to prosper in this world."

"Perhaps—"

"Perhaps you are the spoiled daughter of a man who lived above his means all his life and squandered a family fortune. Perhaps I am left here to tidy the muddle he left behind." Uncle Joseph's voice became crisp. "Your creditors were patient while your mother was alive, not wanting to add to your family's distress. Their patience extended well beyond her death. Due to my efforts, they have extended their generosity even further. But only temporarily. I must warn you, Lavonia, time is short. I advise you to sell your personal possessions and make new living arrangements more suited to a young woman of lesser means. You can't live on Luke's generosity forever, and your allowance is being cut off. Even after those steps are taken, my figures indicate that once everything is sold, there will be very little money left."

Unwilling to accept his proclamation, Lavonia searched for a better solution. "If you could arrange for the merchants I owe to be paid over time, I can manage my expenses."

"They have waited long enough for their money," he said. "Clearly you do not understand the world of business or you would not bother with such ridiculous notions."

"Ridiculous?"

His voice barely concealed his anger. "If you do not wish me to handle your affairs, Lavonia, I can hand them over to my solicitor."

Though she had never met her uncle's solicitor, she conjectured he would be even more disagreeable. "No, Uncle Joseph."

"Then I suggest you not dispute my judgment."

"Yes, Uncle." Lavonia cast her glance to the woven rug. She didn't want him to see the anger flashing in her eyes.

His voice became lighter as he closed his portfolio. "I would suggest that you come and stay with Deidre and me, but we are planning to be abroad most of the season."

Her glance met his. "And how is Aunt Deidre?"

"She is well." His tense expression did not invite further inquiry.

Lavonia wondered at his curt reply. She had only met her uncle's wife of five years once, and she remembered her as homely and unassuming. The family had speculated that Deidre's primary attributes were a respectable family name and a hefty inheritance. Lavonia had heard once that her uncle, in his younger days, had been passionate about a woman, a beauty who had broken off their engagement for an undisclosed reason. Less than a month later, Deidre had entered the Penn family.

Unable to imagine Uncle Joseph feeling ardor for any human, Lavonia doubted the accuracy of the story. In her mind, Deidre, with her money and position, made them the perfect match. "Please send Aunt Deidre my fond regards. I wish you both a pleasant journey abroad. Good day, Uncle Joseph."

His eyes focused their attention back on Lavonia. "Keep in mind what I told you about marriage, Lavonia. A clever match would make your life one of ease." He placed his hat on his balding head with a crisp motion and gave her a curt nod. "Good day."

five

As her uncle closed the parlor door behind him, Lavonia fought the urge to pick up a small marble statue of Venus sitting on a nearby pedestal and hurl it.

"Perhaps you could knock some sense into my uncle, Goddess of Love," Lavonia told the statue. "A clever match indeed! I would never agree to a loveless marriage!"

Through her father's generosity to the poor, Lavonia had witnessed the power of money to help others. Tempting pictures raced through her mind. She imagined what she could accomplish if God granted her control of a fortune. A large Methodist church, perhaps even several churches, could be founded in Georgia using the funds of a wealthy husband. Teachers and Bibles could be brought to America from England to educate the masses so they could read and understand God's word firsthand. Perhaps even a Methodist seminary could be founded.

Shaking her head, she forced the picture of grand churches and happy students out of her mind. "No! I would not marry for money even if I could start ten new churches and finance every circuit rider in America!"

Her anger spent, she folded her arms across her chest. Wrath gave way to guilt as she recalled her sister lying ill in her bedchamber. She struggled for a moment. "No," she whispered. "I could not condemn myself to living a lie. Not even for you, Kitty."

Lavonia mulled over Helen's idea that Vicar Gladstone would make a good husband—both Lavonia and the vicar did aspire to do God's work. She wondered what Uncle

Joseph's reaction would be to her making a match with a clergyman of humble means.

Shuddering, Lavonia remembered her uncle's leering gaze. Though she realized her pride was immodest, she knew his favorable assessment of her appearance to be accurate. Large blue eyes, hair the deepest brown, and a true form were attributes enough to attract the interest of an eligible bachelor. Perhaps even William Amory.

—William Amory! Whatever made him pop into my head?

Closing her eyes, she put her hand to her forehead and tried to suppress the picture of him that kept imposing itself in her mind. In spite of herself, she visualized his clean-cut features, set off by violet eyes and ebony hair. Her heart picked up its pace. Then by sheer determination, she erased his portrait from her thoughts.

I should marry William Amory just to spite my uncle. He would be most displeased with a country doctor who is a struggling artist as well!

Though she compelled herself to let out a light laugh at the prospect, Lavonia could not deceive herself. She knew marriage to William Amory would be no matter of jest.

I can never break my vow to Mama. No matter how much this doctor makes my heart sing, he is Kitty's doctor and nothing more. And that is the way it always shall be.

The chiming clock reminded her that she should tarry no longer in the parlor, so she left without a sound and crept up the stairs to her room. She looked at Kitty's closed bedroom door and decided to keep her conversation with their uncle to herself. Lavonia's faith was powerful enough to sustain her in any financial situation, but Kitty was not as strong, either physically or, Lavonia thought with regret, spiritually.

"For I have learned, in whatsoever state I am, therewith to be content." Saint Paul's words from the fourth chapter of

Philippians had rung in her mind more than once since her parents' deaths.

Glancing at her sister's closed door one last time, Lavonia shook her head. Kitty sought her satisfaction in the pleasures and comforts of this world. *Perhaps it is her sickness that makes her desire comforts so. How do I know? How can I judge her, when I have never been ill a day in my life?*

The sound of Helen's footfalls interrupted her thoughts. Though she quickened her motions, Lavonia failed to duck into her room before Helen called to her, "Lavonia!"

Her hand on the door knob, she turned to face her cousin.

"Lavonia, you look white as snow. Did your meeting with Uncle Joseph not go well?"

"No, it did not." She inhaled, preparing to tell the unhappy truth. "The sale of the house brought next to nothing. The money I thought would allow Katherine and me to live, though modestly, for the rest of our lives, is all but vanished. I have no idea what to do."

"Oh, Lavonia!" Helen's eyes widened, yet she placed a comforting hand on her shoulder. "Fear not, *ma cherie*. You and Katherine may stay here as long as you wish."

Feeling a surge of gratitude, Lavonia embraced Helen. "Thank you. Thank you, Helen."

"Of course you may stay. Was there ever a doubt?"

Breaking away, Lavonia looked her cousin in the eyes. "I know we can stay. But I am sure we shall not be imposing upon your generosity much longer."

The wordless pat on the shoulder Helen gave her before returning downstairs left Levonia with a sense of relief. Yet she knew her problems were far from solved. Sighing, she opened the door to her temporary quarters. Paint the color of a copper roof turned green after weathering was soothing enough to lull her into many nights of dreamless sleep, yet bright enough to keep the room cheerful. The most evident furnishings were a massive four poster canopied bed and a heavy freestanding wardrobe carved in Mahogany wood.

Lavonia remembered both pieces from Helen's room at her parents' home. An inheritance from her great-grandmother, the wood had aged to the color of strong coffee. The feet of both pieces were carved into an eagle's claw clutching a ball. Though a symbol of good luck, the decoration was not to Lavonia's taste. She preferred the simple, smooth lines of the pieces that occupied her bedchamber in Dover.

The remembrance of the little room caused a lump to form in her throat. *I cannot call Dover, nor the house, "home" any longer.*

Eager to distract herself, Lavonia concentrated on a vase of fresh pink and white roses sitting atop a mahogany dressing table. Her cousin always made sure fresh flowers greeted Lavonia each day.

Helen is so thoughtful, so kind. But regardless of how long she insists I stay here, I must not impose myself, nor Kitty and her spells, on Helen and Luke forever.

Sighing, Lavonia made her way to the small chair in front of the basin and splashed lukewarm water onto her face. She thought about her problems as she patted her cheeks and forehead dry with a cotton cloth.

How will I ever find the funds to go to America now? Must I give up my dreams? Must I be left here, forever?

Halting her motions, she looked heavenward and sent a plea to the Lord. *Can it be You do not wish me to work in the mission field, Lord? But how can that be? You have commanded me to honor my father and my mother. Was I wrong to promise Mama I would go? Tell me, Father. What will You have me do?*

She didn't have to wait to realize where her answer could be found. Lavonia rose from her seat and strode to the bed. Sitting on the cotton bedspread, she picked up the Bible that had been waiting for her on the night table. Closing her eyes, she said a silent prayer for God's direction before turning to a page.

The leather-bound volume, worn from many hours of contemplation, opened to Matthew 6:19. "Lay not up for yourselves treasures upon earth, where moth and rust doth corrupt, and where thieves break through and steal. But lay up for yourselves treasures in heaven, where neither moth nor rust doth corrupt, and where thieves do not break through nor steal: For where your treasure is, there will your heart be also."

Closing the Bible, Lavonia uttered a whispered prayer. "Search my heart, dear Lord. Give me the strength to serve You according to Your will."

ૐ

William Amory looked about the London office of Cuthbert Whittington, Esquire. The room was furnished in an embarrassment of expense. Purple draperies of the finest velvet covered each of the four windows. Several botanical oil paintings and ornate gold sconces decorated each expansive wall, which was covered in thick wallpaper depicting scenes of city life. Crown molding imported from Italy offered eye-catching accents. Woolen Oriental rugs added color to burnished wooden floors. A massive desk was the room's centerpiece. William guessed moving the piece of furniture would require the efforts of six men. Through his medical practice and commissioned portraits, William was accustomed to calling upon the wealthy. Yet he didn't feel at ease enough to take a seat on any of the four velvet-covered chairs.

Sighing, he wished he were home or visiting the sick. Specifically, Katherine Penn. He swallowed, knowing full well he didn't want to admit he really wished to see not his new patient, but her sister, Lavonia.

Lavonia. Lavonia Penn. His thoughts sang out her name

over and over, seldom leaving him for long. No other woman had ever had such a stunning effect upon him, and assuredly not after just one meeting. Easily summoning her image to his mind, he lingered upon her deep brown tresses, so rich and lustrous, their color would shame Cuthbert Whittington's gleaming mahogany desk. A smile touched his lips as he recalled Lavonia's expressive blue eyes. How exciting they were, flashing anger in one moment, and swimming with pools of compassion the next. How genuine and fearless were her soft pink lips, unafraid to speak the truth. And, though he was aware that a gentleman shouldn't entertain such thoughts, his mind drifted to her curves, so sumptuous they couldn't be concealed even beneath a dour mourning dress.

He gave himself a mental whipping for harboring such thoughts about the comely Miss Lavonia Penn. After all, she was determined to be a missionary. She had told him in no uncertain terms that she desired not to marry, but to serve the Son of God, Jesus Christ.

William forced her image to melt into oblivion. He couldn't ask Lavonia to change her mind, not when her cause was so noble, so right. Perhaps her goodness was part of the attraction. William sighed. Of course it was. And that was exactly why he had to stop thinking about her.

"Daydreaming, Mr. Amory?" Cuthbert Whittington's voice was sharp enough to refocus William's thoughts on business.

William tilted his head in greeting. "I beg your pardon, but that is *Dr.* Amory." He kept his voice brisk.

"Very well, Doctor." Looking down a long nose, the solicitor seemed to be passing down unfavorable judgment. Motioning for William to take a seat, he took his place behind the desk. "I regret a prior engagement shall keep me from lingering here," he said in a manner most unconvincing.

"I understand."

"Good. Now then, you are aware that your benefactor,

Philemon Midas, was a man of considerable wealth?"

"Since he could afford to be a benefactor, I assumed Mr. Midas was wealthy, yes."

"But you never met Mr. Midas?" he asked, his voice hopeful.

"No, a fact I find most grievous, though I consented not to meet in accordance with his wishes. I always wanted to thank him in person for his generosity."

"Indeed. As did the many others he helped."

Becoming impatient, William said, "I am a busy man, Mr. Whittington. I hope you did not summon me all the way here merely to tell me you have a secret that I am not privy to."

"Of course not." The solicitor looked vexed. "I have some papers I need you to sign."

"Why? Certainly I am not entitled to any portion of his estate."

Cuthbert Whittington smiled, though the expression did not reach his eyes. "I am pleased you understand that. Not all of Mr. Midas's beneficiaries do." He let out a weary sigh. "But unfortunately, that is a matter for me to settle. In the meantime," he said, handing William a document, "certainly you will have no objection to signing this."

A quick read of the contents revealed that William was being asked to forego any claims to the Midas fortune. Having no plans to ask the estate for additional funds, he acquiesced and signed the waiver.

Moments later, William stepped into a brisk spring breeze. Caught off guard by a burst of wind, he clutched his light morning coat more tightly to his chest. The solicitor's request had come as no surprise, but the duplicate of the waiver he held in his black leather valise was tangible evidence that his life had changed forever.

six

Days passed as Lavonia waited for Kitty to recover from her recurring headaches enough to get out of bed. Helen provided good company and pleasant diversions. Yet in Helen's absence, Lavonia jockeyed between worry about the future and intruding thoughts about William Amory. Though she concealed the fact from her hostess and tried to deny it to herself, Lavonia was eager to see the doctor upon his next visit.

Finally, during a midday meal of roast pork and Yorkshire pudding, her sister made an appearance in the dining room. Her dark hair was set in a stylish coil and she had exchanged her black mourning dress for a lavender frock.

"I am so pleased to see you up and about again," Lavonia welcomed her.

"As am I," Luke added before instructing a servant to set an additional place at the table.

Delight was obvious on Helen's face. "Your appearance for luncheon must mean you are feeling well now, Katherine?"

"Not very." Letting out a dramatic sigh, Katherine sank into the chair positioned in front of the empty plate.

"Obviously you feel strong enough to rise from bed," Lavonia noted. Her sister was always slow to recover from a spell, usually citing the bloodletting process as the cause. However, Dr. Amory had not bled her, so Lavonia believed her strength should be making its way back more quickly than in the past.

I pray Dr. Amory knows what he is doing. Perhaps Kitty should have been bled, just as the others doctors are wont to do. Lavonia closed her eyes for a moment. *Dear Lord, please keep Kitty from becoming increasingly ill.*

"I see you are praying for me." Katherine turned to Helen. "It is a wonder I am not fit as a fiddle, since Lavonia consistently keeps me in her prayers."

"And so she should," Luke observed. "What was Osmond telling us in his sermon last week? Something about praying without ceasing?"

Lavonia could not resist a retort. "Indeed, when Vicar Gladstone prays, it appears as though he will never cease!"

Luke threw her a chastising look. Helen let out a titter and Katherine looked perplexed.

"My apologies for making a joke at your friend's expense, Luke." Lavonia set her countenance into a serious demeanor. "I always enjoy a sermon on 1 Timothy 5:17. All of us would be well advised to adhere to the words of Saint Paul."

"If only they worked. I really do not feel much better at all," Katherine insisted. "In fact, being forced to wear this old dress now that I am finally out of mourning clothes only serves to add to my poor temper."

Casting a disdainful look upon the pretty frock, Katherine added her best pout. Recalling the doctor's diagnosis, Lavonia at once realized she had seen this tactic employed upon her father a number of times. Many new dresses, hats, shoes, and even a trip abroad had been the fruits of her efforts. *No, the doctor's diagnosis must have me imagining the most peculiar things. He has to be wrong about Kitty. He just has to be!*

"Really," Katherine told Helen, "I do not know how much longer I could have abided wearing those horrible old black dresses. I know I must respect Mama and Papa, but Papa especially would not have wanted me to suffer."

Lavonia chose that moment to take a long sip of tea. *How will she react when I tell her we can afford no new clothing at all?*

"There is no need for you to worry, Katherine. I shall make an appointment with my dressmaker and have several new gowns sewn for you. And Lavonia as well," Helen reassured.

Lavonia cringed upon seeing how Katherine beguiled her hostess with barely any effort on her part. Yet she was not ready to condemn her sister. *Surely Kitty does not intentionally trick and manipulate others. Like a little child, she merely wants her way.*

Her sister's eyes shone. "Just contemplating a new dress sends me into a favorable temper."

Though it pained her to dampen the mood, Lavonia knew she must. "Your offer is quite generous, Helen, but we have a fine selection of dresses suitably subdued for this stage of mourning."

"Oh, Lavonia," Katherine protested. "Must you always be so practical?"

"I fear I must."

"Then you must be hiding some bad news from me." Turning her attention to Helen, Katherine gave her cousin a look designed to garner sympathy. "You can surmise why I thought it wise to lunch with you. My sister will not confide in me when I am ill. I am aware our uncle was here on business. Five days have passed, and still I know nothing about what was said between them."

"Let me take the burden of worry on my shoulders," Lavonia offered.

"You need not make such sacrifices, my sister. Though I am cursed with sickness, I desire to be informed about my future."

"Very well."

Helen and Luke rose from their chairs, obviously intent on exiting to offer the sisters privacy. But Lavonia raised her hand, causing them to stop. "You are our closest family and have shown us nothing but kindness since our parents' deaths. Please remain here. There need not be secrets between us."

The newlyweds exchanged curious looks then returned to their seats at either end of the table.

"Both of you have been more than charitable and benevolent to provide us obliging accommodation in our time of distress. We are both grateful to you," Lavonia began. "But because of the small sum the sale of our house brought, we cannot repay you. Therefore, we must be leaving so I may seek gainful employment elsewhere."

"Small sum?" Katherine's voice shook. "Do you mean to say we are. . .poor?"

Unwilling to encourage an outburst, Lavonia kept her voice firm. "Yes."

"Such drastic action is not necessary," Helen said. "I meant what I said earlier. There is no hurry." Apparently thinking Katherine would be more easily persuaded to stay, Helen turned to her. "You must remain at least long enough for Dr. Amory to find a cure for your headaches."

"No. We shall be leaving tomorrow," Lavonia proclaimed.

"Tomorrow? Why so soon?"

"As you have noticed, the doctor has not returned in the five days since his first visit with Katherine. I surmise he will not be making another call. I fear he may have been put off."

"Put off? Whatever for?"

Lavonia felt her face flush with chagrin. Bowing her head, she muttered, "I called him a charlatan."

"Au contraire." Helen let out a laugh. "A charlatan? How droll! Our doctor does have modern ideas, but I do not believe I have ever heard anyone call him such. If only I could have seen his face when you displayed such a spirited disposition."

Lavonia winced when she remembered her reaction to the doctor telling her she was being manipulated by her sister. "I doubt he would share your humor."

"I fancy the doctor was not offended, but scared to death," Helen smirked.

"Scared?"

Helen giggled. "Though I do not wish to offend you, I must say you were *la flirteuse* with our good doctor the last time the two of you met. Why, you practically asked him to marry you!"

"Really? My devout sister exhibited romantic inclinations?" Katherine's voice dripped with sarcasm. She batted her eyes at Lavonia. "Though I must ask, did you propose before or after you called him a charlatan?"

A heated flush rose from the base of Lavonia's neck to the top of her hair line as she disputed Helen's account. *"Exaggère tu!"*

"Vraiment? I have never seen you play *la coquette* as you did with our poor doctor." She gave Lavonia an indulgent smile. "Flirt if you must, but William Amory is not the one for you, my dear cousin."

"And why not?" Lavonia blurted.

"Perhaps I should pose a question to you. How much do you know about William Amory?"

"Not much, I admit. But at least the doctor and I have been properly introduced. I could not say the same about my secret admirer only a few days ago, and yet you were set to betroth us."

Helen was about to reply when a visitor interrupted.

"Did I hear someone speak of a betrothal?"

Lavonia needed not turn to know the voice belonged to the vicar in question.

"Osmond!" Luke rose to welcome his friend. "I had no idea you were here."

"I knocked at the door, but no one answered. I beg your pardon for entering unannounced, but as an old friend, I feel I am privileged to take such liberties."

"Indeed you are. Although for your expediency in the future, I shall instruct the servants to be more alert to the prospect of visitors knocking upon our front door. In the meantime, do join us for luncheon."

"Luncheon?" A partially carved pork resting in a pool of dark brown gravy on a platter in the center of the table offered ample evidence that a meal was in progress. He let his eyes rove over the meat and the remaining Yorkshire pudding as though he had only then discovered their existence. "Oh, my!" With a flair of his hand, he withdrew his pocket watch from his vest. "I've come at a bad time—I did not realize it was noon."

Helen was seated close enough to Lavonia to whisper sarcastically, "Oh my! What a surprise, *n'est pas?*"

Lavonia covered her grin with her napkin in a show of wiping her lips. Having invoked Luke's ire with one insult directed at Osmond, she dared not laugh aloud at Helen's astute observation.

Surveying the dinner party as he returned his watch to its pocket, the vicar allowed a look of dreamlike rapture to cross his features. "Performing my tasks as a member of the clergy offers such great reward. The morning hours fly by as if they are but a moment in eternity."

Helen whispered, "Unlike his Sunday sermons."

"Please!" All Lavonia's willpower was required to control the outburst of laughter that threatened.

"Pray tell, of whose betrothal were you speaking when I arrived?" He tilted his head toward Katherine. "Perhaps you are the future bride, Miss, Miss. . .?"

"Forgive my negligence," Luke apologized. "This is Miss Katherine Penn, our dear Lavonia's sister. Regrettably, the younger Miss Penn has been too ill to attend Sunday morning worship services with us."

"Regrettably, indeed," he agreed, his voice lilting on the last syllable. The vicar studied Katherine as if he were charmed by her appearance. "I trust you are feeling better?"

"I feel quite well now, thank you, Vicar."

"Then allow me," Luke interrupted. "Vicar Osmond Gladstone, this is Miss Katherine Penn."

"*Enchantè,* Miss Penn." To Lavonia's amazement, the vicar's voice seemed soft and inviting.

Looking down at the meal of which she had partaken little, Katherine blushed as a little smile reached her lips. Lavonia wasn't sure whether her reaction was one of genuine shyness or if she was acting coy. Regardless, the vicar seemed to be enjoying himself.

As soon as the servant set yet another place at the table, Osmond stood before the chair and asked, "Might I add my blessing?"

"We would be pleased if you would do so," Luke responded.

The vicar cleared his throat and began to speak. "Father in heaven, we give our thanks for this exquisite meal of which we are about to partake. We thank You for the delectable roast pork and a delicious Yorkshire pudding, along with vegetables You created, cheeses of all descriptions, fresh fruit made by Your hands, which shall be enriched by generous portions of premium clotted cream, wonderful yeast rolls accompanied by fruit jams and creamy butter, and the rich tea for which our great nation is known and loved, all prepared by faithful and devoted servants, as well as for the scrumptious dessert that will conclude this excellent luncheon. We are grateful that You have seen fit to shower us with Your blessings, as shown by the prestigious company we are keeping among us today, the well-appointed home in which we are privileged to dine, the fair and fine ladies who, by their very presence, enrich the lives of men by allowing us to drink in their beauty, not unlike the most exotic and exquisite flowers, and the charming and gracious host whom You have blessed with the prosperity he assuredly deserves, and for the agreeable disposition he possesses, which allows him a willingness to share with me, his devoted and lifelong friend, the finest food available in all the land. We pray that all of us dining here today shall retain Your good favor, and that You shall continue to find us worthy of the superlative comforts Your creation has to offer. Amen." Opening his eyes, the vicar beamed with obvious self-satisfaction.

"That was the most beautiful blessing I have ever heard in all my life," Katherine said in a voice just above a whisper.

Aware that her sister seldom employed hyperbole, Lavonia snapped her head in Katherine's direction. An angelic look had overtaken her features, emphasizing their loveliness.

"It is so wonderful that you happened by." If she realized the timing was the vicar's ploy to dine with them, she gave no indication.

"It is lovely, indeed. I only hope I did not interrupt a private discussion. Although, since I am a member of the clergy," he noted, eyeing Katherine, "any confidence you wish to share with me will naturally be kept under the darkest cloak of secrecy."

"We were simply discussing Lavonia's visit with Uncle Joseph," Katherine revealed.

The flush from her praise drained from his face. The vicar remained uncharacteristically silent, stabbing at the meat with his fork as though he wished to butcher it a second time.

Katherine did not seem to notice. "He is settling our parents' estate."

"Then you should be quite well spoken for," Osmond observed, though his terse tone of voice indicated otherwise. "He has the reputation of being quite the shrewd businessman."

"So he continues to remind me," Lavonia quipped. "Though he offers little proof."

The vicar glanced at her. "I noticed at luncheon the other day that he seems to be acquainted with Dr. Amory?"

Lavonia's stomach felt as though it were flipping upon the mere mention of the doctor's name. "Apparently, although I know nothing about their relationship." Lavonia wished she had queried William about why her uncle's arrival so disturbed him. She decided to seize the opportunity to discover more. "Luke, what do you know about them?"

Her host shook his head. "Nothing. I was not even aware of their acquaintance. Were you, Helen?"

"No. But I fail to see why it matters."

"I suppose it matters not." The vicar shrugged and let out a chuckle that seemed to be forced. "Perhaps I am so accustomed to my role as a clergyman that I show concern for everyone as if they are all members of my flock."

"But as Christians, are we not to show concern for our fellow pilgrims in the faith?" Lavonia challenged. "Recall Jesus' words in John 13:34–35: 'A new commandment I give unto you, That ye love one another; as I have loved you, that ye also love one another. By this shall all men know that ye are my disciples, if ye have love one to another.'"

"Saint Paul also cautions us twice, in 2 Timothy 3:11, and again in 1 Timothy 5:13, that we shall not be busybodies," said the vicar.

"Passages you would do well to review, no doubt." Though Lavonia knew her comment was ungracious, bathed in rile, she did not regret voicing her opinion.

The vicar gave her a disagreeable look. "Then perhaps I should refrain from recommending that a woman from a family of stature and means such as yourself should not employ one, but two, business advisors."

"Really? Do you think that would be most politic?" Katherine said sincerely, her eyes widened as though she were a small child just entrusted with the keys to wisdom.

Osmond's chest puffed when he realized the younger sister was entranced by his every word. "I fear I do not command great knowledge of financial affairs, but am imparting what is merely recognized as common sense."

"Lavonia and Katherine would do well to heed your words of advice," Luke agreed.

Emboldened by the encouragement, Osmond added, "And if Dr. Amory has close connections with any businessman in whom you do not have the utmost conviction, I would seek the services of another doctor."

"Are you saying my uncle and Dr. Amory are dishonest?" Katherine asked.

Her unvarnished candor left the vicar flustered. "Miss Penn,

I assure you, I would make no such assumptions. Why, I know very little about either man."

Indeed, Lavonia mused to herself. *That, my dear vicar, shall remain to be seen.*

ૐ

William Amory stirred his soup. The motion caused the corn and peas to travel through broth that remained flavorless despite the few bits of salted ham that constituted a serving of meat. The salt and pepper made their way around the long table at Mrs. Potter's boarding establishment as each lodger shook a few grains of each into the soup in hopes of adding life to the listless meal.

"You simply cannot take two pieces of bread, Mr. Barron," Miss Goodwin protested.

"Is that right?" he answered, his bulbous lips puffing into a pout. Tilting his head toward William, he murmured, " 'Tis no wonder she's an old maid, the battle-ax!"

"I heard that," Mrs. Ford scolded. "Miss Goodwin is right. If you take two portions of bread, there shan't be enough for everyone. Do you not agree, Dr. Amory?" The older woman cast him a smile as attractive as possible for a woman whose best days were last seen during the revolt of the American colonies.

William plastered on his best smile for her. For once, he was grateful for her interference. The soup would hardly be satisfactory to keep his stomach from griping until the following morning's breakfast. For a lady, he would have relinquished his serving of bread, but he wasn't willing to be as generous with the obese Mr. Barron. "Of course, if the platter contains only one portion for each of us. Simple mathematics."

Snarling, Mr. Barron hurled the bread back onto the platter. "Make us another batch, will you, Mrs. Potter?"

The skinny woman shook her head in the negative, though not with enough vigor to shake loose any gray hairs from her severe coiffure. "For a pound a week, that is all the bread you get. You should be obliged to me for such a bargain, and cease your grumbling."

"Is there dessert?" Mr. Barron wanted to know.

"Not with the price of sugar at the market. You'll have to wait 'til Sunday."

A round of resigned sighs fluttered around the table. Mr. Barron threw his napkin into his empty bowl. "I'll be at the tavern for a round of stout, I will. Mebbe a stiff brew will stick to me ribs." He tossed his head in William's direction. "How's about you, Doc?"

"No, thank you."

He shrugged. "Suit yerself."

After dinner, William climbed the steep, narrow set of stairs to the third floor. The rented room was so depressing, he almost wished he had accepted Mr. Barron's invitation. Paint that had once been white had turned a light shade of gray from smoke that belched from the fireplace. Next to the fireplace stood his easel, which held an unfinished portrait and his box of paints. The floor, spotted and stained from years of abuse, creaked in several places no matter how softly he walked. At least on this night, he wouldn't have to endure the wrath of Mr. Barron's broom tapping on his ceiling below in protest to the noise.

A single bed made of dented knotted pine held a hard mattress. It, along with a wardrobe housing the few garments he owned, consumed most of his allotted space. The only piece of furniture William could call his own was an oak rolltop desk and comfortable secretary's chair, a purchase made only after scrimping for a year. Sitting in the chair, William opened the desk and extracted a small box from one of the cubicles.

Inside the box was a diminutive silver ring. William had not taken it from its place in such a long time he had almost forgotten what it looked like, how the cold silver warmed in his hand. The ring was the only memento he had from his mother, a woman he had never met. The engraving on the delicate band read *Vous et nul autre*.

You and no other. He wondered about the adolescent girl who had worn this ring, and the young man who had given it to her. "Such promise. The beauty of such a sentiment. If only my father had stood by his promise. How different my life would have been." He sighed. "I shall never let a woman I love suffer."

A long-forgotten Bible verse popped into his head. *"There-fore shall a man leave his father and his mother, and shall cleave unto his wife: and they shall be one flesh."*

At that moment he realized why he had wanted to contemplate the ring. For once, he had met a woman who deserved to wear it. How he wished he could give her the ring.

He imagined Lavonia in his embrace as he buried his face in her deep brown hair, inhaling without inhibition the scent of roses that engulfed her being. For an eternity, he wanted to look into her eyes, as blue as any artist's fanciful rendition of the Thames River. He wished he could touch her skin—it brought to mind the smooth cream he poured over fresh strawberries, the color of her lips.

William didn't want to indulge in his fantasy, but he was certain that Lavonia too was as affected by his presence as he was hers. When they were together, he saw interest in her eyes, noticed the tension in her body. If her unspoken reaction had not been proof to satisfy, Helen's admonishment at Lavonia's verbal sparring demonstrated well her response to him.

But Helen's chastisement also showed William that Lavonia's cousin did not sanction a future between them. William knew all too well how difficult her disapproval would be to conquer. Yet he knew he could, in time. His own mistake would be more difficult to surmount. His assessment of Katherine's ailment had angered Lavonia, and she had not bothered to conceal her feelings.

"Why did I choose to be honest?" he mused. "And what was my reward? To be labeled a charlatan."

William indulged in a smile. "I wonder if that is what she really thinks of me? She seemed a bit less frosty at the noon meal, at least until her uncle arrived."

William felt the smile melt from his face. "Lavonia seemed to like Joseph even less than I do. I wonder why."

He was well aware of the source of Joseph's animosity toward him. Thinking back to another time and circumstance, William remembered a pretty blonde who had once anticipated becoming Mrs. Joseph Penn.

ᘒ

"You are looking especially well today, Miss Hawthorne. You are proving to be a fine muse."

Rather than being flattered, his subject huffed, raising her nose heavenward. "Must I remind you I am engaged? I am here to have my portrait painted, not to become your paramour."

William could not conceal his surprise upon hearing such an accusation. "I beg your pardon. My sentiment was not expressed with such intent."

"So you say." Susanna repositioned herself in the stiff chair. "You would do well to remember that my fiancé is paying for the picture you paint. I have no need to tell you he is the richest man in the province. As Mrs. Joseph Penn, I shall be well situated." Her gray eyes narrowed. "I need not the attentions of a struggling artist, no matter how he might flatter me with words and a pleasing portrait."

Pretending to ignore her tirade, William touched the brush to a fold in the green dress on the canvas and listened to her argument. Though Susanna was a skilled actress, the tiniest bit of regret in her voice portrayed that she was not as ecstatic about her engagement as her words indicated. "So you meet your wedding day with great anticipation?" He lifted his eyes enough to catch a glimpse of doubt cross her face.

"Indeed, I, I—" A tear streamed from her left eye. "I do not!" With that, she buried her face in her cupped hands and burst into tears. The sound of her sobbing rang throughout the studio. Her shoulders shook with emotion.

Seeing her distress, William dropped his brush and ran to her side. Kneeling beside the chair, he withdrew a kerchief from his pocket and handed it to the weeping woman. "I beg your pardon. A thousand times, I beg your pardon. I never meant to force a confidence from you."

His apology seemed to calm her. She blew her nose into the kerchief with a zeal he was unaccustomed to seeing in a lady, an act that resulted in loud honking sounds reminiscent of a flock of geese. "I have spent so much time with you, Dr. Amory. Or might I call you 'William'?" She didn't wait for his reply. "I have heard such things. Such awful things."

William's heart felt as though it was sinking in his chest. He had heard about Joseph Penn and his sly business dealings. Could it be that Susanna had heard about them as well? Aloud he asked, "What have you heard?"

"Oh, it is just awful!" A fresh wave of sobs ensued. Between gasps, she asked, "How can I marry someone so dishonest?"

Before he could answer, she threw herself upon his chest, not waiting for a verbal invitation or for him to extend his arms for an embrace. Helpless to arise since he was still on his knees, William was trapped. There was nothing he could do when he heard the door to his studio open. His unexpected visitor had not bothered to knock, but had burst in and was surveying the studio.

"I say! What have we here?"

Susanna seemed oblivious to how they must have looked, since she made no attempt to release her embrace. Gently taking her arms from around himself, William placed them in her lap and rose to his feet. The man he faced was a fellow boarder. "We have nothing here, Samuel. At least nothing that is of your concern."

"Nothin'? It seemed to be somethin', what with the lady sobbin' and all that. You can hear her carryin' on all the way to the front stoop, you can." His voice was slurred, the result of too many pints of lager.

"I beg your pardon for the disturbance. But as you can see, she is quite all right." He looked at Susanna, who gave a vigorous nod in agreement.

Their assurances did little to appease their accuser. The portly man had a glimmer in his eye. "Looks like you're doin' a little more than paintin' here, that's what I say. I wouldn't want to be in your shoes when Mr. Penn finds out about this. That I wouldn't." He let out an evil laugh before making a hasty departure, slamming the door behind him.

Samuel's prophecy proved true, in no small part because he spread the word about what he thought he had seen among those who frequented the local tavern.

❧

"How wrong he was!" William mused, bringing himself back to the present. "Yet I am paying for the gossip and innuendo, even now." He felt sorry for Joseph Penn—the man had obviously suffered much since that difficult time. William didn't blame him for his ill will toward him. He imagined he would feel much the same given the elder Penn's circumstances.

William let out a sigh. Joseph Penn had no way of knowing how much closer William had come to God since then. There was a good reason for William's change of heart and of attitude.

For the Lord had saved William's life.

seven

"Good morning, Dr. Amory." Having stopped midway in her descent of the curved mahogany staircase on the left side of the Syms' foyer, Lavonia was in the perfect position for William to observe her.

She was even more lovely than he remembered. Her beauty seemed a phantasm of his most elaborate imaginings. Dark ringlets framed her face in a fashionable coiffure that complemented her delicate features. Her high-necked morning dress was styled in a manner he had not seen in several years, yet it accentuated her form, its lavender hue contrasting with her blue eyes, reminding him of blue and purple pansies.

He managed to sound professional with a mere, "Good morning, Miss Penn."

Lavonia gave a nod of dismissal to the maid who had answered the door. The girl exited and Lavonia descended the rest of the stairs. "I was wondering when you might call upon Katherine again."

Could this mean she wanted to see me again?

Despite his hopes, William was not ready to reveal his emotions just yet. "Were you? I feared I should not return at all, since you seemed so apprehensive about entrusting your sister's care to that of a charlatan."

To his satisfaction, Lavonia's face flushed an enchanting shade of red. "Having taken time since then to contemplate your diagnosis, Doctor, I now perceive that perhaps your opinion is justified."

William's eyebrows rose, only this time in surprise. "Is that so? Would you care to elaborate?"

"No." As if regretting her abrupt answer, Lavonia added, "I trust you are not offended that I am not taking you into my full confidence. I need not remind you that we have known each other only briefly."

"I am never one to force a confidence, Miss Penn. Although I hope you would not jeopardize the health of your sister, or of yourself, by keeping secrets." William hoped his face did not betray his disappointment. He wished she would trust him, but he knew it probably was too soon in their friendship.

"I do trust you, Dr. Amory."

Smiling, he gave her a nod. "I am glad to hear that."

"When I feel it would benefit all of us for me to share my observations, I shall not hesitate," she said with a convincing smile.

"I do hope my new patient is feeling better."

"Well enough to leave her bedchamber and to pursue her needlework once more." Lavonia cocked her head toward the back of the house. "She is in the drawing room."

"Excellent. May I speak with her?"

"But of course." Walking toward the back of the house, Lavonia motioned for him to follow her.

Transparent glass in the French doors revealed a different young woman than he had visited earlier in the week. Katherine was sitting in an overstuffed chair, embroidering pink flowers onto a kerchief. The peaceful look on her countenance suggested she had not a care in the world. The sound of Lavonia's light footfalls brought her to attention.

"Vonnie! Has the morning mail arrived? I do so hope there's another letter from Aunt Amelia."

Lavonia shook her head. "You have a visitor."

Her eyes lit with obvious anticipation as she leapt from her chair, allowing her needlework to fall to the floor. Her gaze fell upon the doctor. "Oh. It is you, Dr. Amory." The expectation drained from her voice.

He nodded toward her. "Good morning, Miss Penn."

"Good morning." She returned to her seat, her face reddening as she retrieved the fallen needlework.

"I am pleased to see you are feeling well enough to be up."

Katherine put her hand to her forehead in an affected motion. "*Oui*. But it is such a strain to be out of bed. I am feeling quite weak this morning."

"Really, Kitty?" Lavonia's voice indicated a combination of concern and surprise. "That is not what you have been reporting to me."

"Oh, dear Vonnie, I have indeed been feeling exceedingly poorly. My head has been aching every day, though not as much as it was the day Dr. Amory saw me before."

"Why did you not tell me?"

Katherine shot Lavonia a look that was enough to induce guilt in a saint. "I have been so very much trouble for you already, I did not wish to cause you, or Helen and Luke, who have been so very kind to me, further anxiety."

"How considerate of you," William couldn't resist observing.

Katherine focused her gaze on him. "It has been so very long since you have come to call on me, Doctor. I surmised you had forgotten all about me and my illness."

"*Au contraire*, Miss Penn. I would have gladly called upon you, but I have been on business in London. I returned only last night."

"I hope you will not be on business too long in the future." Placing a hand on her chest, she explained, "I never know when a spell might come on."

"I assure you, I shall do what I can to ease your pain."

"I thank you," Katherine said in a withering voice.

Ignoring her implied dismissal, William chose to give his patient some sound advice. "You might discover your head will feel better if you keep yourself out of drafts."

"This room is hardly drafty, Doctor," Katherine argued.

"How can it be, now that spring has arrived?"

"There is still a bit of breeze circulating through the house, whether or not you notice it. And the spring air is cool enough to require you to be prudent. A precaution you might take is to cover your shoulders with a shawl, particularly when you choose to wear a dress that does not cover the neck and barely conceals the shoulders."

"I shall thank you to keep your observations to yourself," Katherine snapped.

Lavonia turned to William. "I beg pardon for my sister's sour humor. I suppose by now you are quite aware that her headaches cause her to suffer from an ill disposition as well as physical pain."

"That is quite all right. As a doctor, I rarely see a patient at his—or her—best."

At that moment, a white longhaired cat leapt onto Katherine's lap. "Out of here, you beast! You'll ruin my needlework!" With an abrupt motion, she picked up the offending creature by the scruff of the neck and tossed it aside, where it landed on the floor on all fours then dashed out of the room.

"I see your sister is fond of pets," William observed to Lavonia.

Lavonia's mouth curled into a knowing grin. "Quite fond, indeed."

At that moment, Katherine let out a series of sneezes. Lavonia acted quickly to hand her a kerchief.

"Does she sneeze like that often?"

"I never noticed Katherine experiencing sneezing fits before we arrived here."

William thought for a moment. "You have never lived with a household pet?"

"No. Mama was not markedly enthusiastic about animals."

"Have Katherine's headaches increased since she arrived here?"

"Come to think of it, they have." Lavonia nodded.

"Then I surmise she should not be residing with an indoor cat."

By this time, Katherine had recovered enough from her sneezing to speak. "Dr. Amory, I would thank you to interview me rather than my sister about my condition. It is I, rather than she, who is your patient."

"I beg your pardon, Miss Penn."

"I will have you to know that Snowball has nothing to do with my headaches, if that is what you are implying," she objected. "I like it here, and I am not leaving until I must."

"I implied nothing of the sort," William assured her. "I am merely suggesting that if one sneezes when near a creature, then perhaps one should avoid contact with it. And from what I have seen, that would not be a regrettable course of action from your viewpoint."

Katherine's eyes narrowed. "If you are quite through with your visit, Dr. Amory, I would like to wish you a good day."

"And a good day to you, Miss Penn." William tried to keep his voice pleasant, no small feat considering Katherine's rancorous temper.

"I shall see the doctor to the door," Lavonia informed Katherine.

"To discuss me, no doubt."

"No doubt."

When they were beyond earshot of the drawing room, Lavonia asked, "Do you have any advice for me, Dr. Amory?"

"Yes. Encourage any suitor who might present himself. The prospect of romance might be just the thing to improve her temper." He flashed her a smile to indicate he was only half serious.

Lavonia let out a pleasant giggle. "Perhaps. Do you think her headaches would disappear as well?"

William turned serious. "That is hard to say."

"You do believe she suffers from headaches?"

"Yes. But I noticed their extent and severity ebbs and flows according to how pleased she is with her present circumstances."

"For example?"

"Did you not notice how serene she looked while she was alone, doing her needlework? It was only when she saw us that she became pale and started to complain."

"But even you admitted she really does suffer," Lavonia pointed out. "Is there nothing you can do for her?"

"Her circumstances can be controlled to a degree. And as you heard me caution her, she must stay out of drafts and away from the cat. But beyond giving her that advice, there may not be much I can do."

"If only something could be done. I hate to see her suffer."

Studying Lavonia's face and the hurt in her expression, William remembered afresh why he was attracted to Lavonia for more than her physical beauty. Her compassion and concern for others, plus her strong spirit, drew him to her.

"I regret I cannot linger, Dr. Amory," Lavonia said, snapping him back to the present. "I promised I would appear at the church at ten this morning to help roll bandages for the hospital. I shall be late if I tarry."

For the first time, he noticed she had been carrying a shawl in the crook of her arm. He was comforted to realize she was not feigning a reason to depart.

"I wish I were not visiting my patients this morning, so I could help as well."

"I wish you could, too." As she looked into his eyes, her expression revealed she would welcome his presence beyond providing an extra pair of hands.

Without words, William swept toward her and extended his hands for her shawl so he could assist her in wrapping the garment around her shoulders. Though she complied by surrendering the wrap, crocheted in lavender wool, he stopped in mid motion.

As soon as Lavonia noticed, she asked, "Is something amiss, Dr. Amory?"

"No. I mean, yes." Stammering was so unlike him, he felt like a schoolboy.

Her face softened from mild alarm to a look of amusement. "Do tell."

William looked about the drafty foyer, which at once managed to be both massive and practical, much too practical for his mission. "Might I ask you into the parlor?"

Lavonia's eyes moved leftward, long enough to note the time on the grandfather clock. She seemed to debate the merits of staying versus attending her church meeting on time. To his pleasure, she decided to stay. "All right."

William turned to one side and with a sweeping motion of his hand, invited Lavonia to enter the adjacent room before him. Taking his cue, she entered the parlor and situated herself on one side of the mahogany bench.

"May I?"

Answering her affirmative nod, he sat beside her. Closer than ever to her, he inhaled a whiff of the rose scent that he had begun to associate with her. As he delighted in the aroma and the vision of Lavonia, he looked into her eyes. "I have a confession to make. Though I did want to see your sister, I had another reason for calling today."

"Another reason?"

"I have something for you."

"For me?"

He nodded. His heart rate increased and he suddenly felt nervous. Swallowing, he withdrew a white slip of paper. "I wrote this last night."

Lifting his gaze to Lavonia's face for an instant, he saw her blue eyes widen with curiosity and—was it?—anticipation.

He felt his stomach lurch in a way it hadn't since his adolescent years. He almost wished he hadn't mentioned the poem to Lavonia, but her intense stare told him it was too late to change his mind.

He began reading the small, well-formed cursive letters:

I met an angel here today
  Comforting her sister's heart.
She knew not that she pierced mine own.
  Or how it cries when we must part—

William looked upon Lavonia with a bat of his eyelid, enough time to gauge her response, yet not long enough to let her speak. Her milky features, already soft, had grown even more so. Her eyes were so alight, they seemed to contain all the stars in a midnight sky. Her pink lips were parted as if they wanted to taste his sweet words. Well-kept hands were clasped to her chest, making him wonder if they were trying to hold his poem in her heart.

Her obviously favorable response gave him courage. He had opened his mouth to begin the second stanza when he heard Helen's voice.

"Stop right there, Doctor."

Both of them snapped their heads in Helen's direction. She was standing in the doorway of the parlor, her arms folded across her chest, concealing part of the bodice on her sky blue morning dress.

"What, pray tell, is happening here?"

As if the motion would strengthen her, Lavonia stood. "William was just reading me a poem—"

"A poem?" She paused. "By whom?"

Feeling the tension, William opted for levity. "Certainly not Shakespeare."

Helen's narrowed eyes indicated she was in no mood for

humor. "If what I heard is any indication, I quite agree." She cut her glance to Lavonia. "Would you like to tell me what has been happening here?"

Lavonia shrugged. "The doctor was merely reading me a bit of poetry." Her voice was pitched an octave higher than normal.

"Please, let there be no trouble here." William rose from his seat as he folded the paper and returned it to his pocket. "Forgive me for upsetting you, Mrs. Syms. That was never my intent."

"Perhaps that was not your intent, but it was certainly the result! I will not have you toying with my cousin." Turning to one side, she motioned for him to leave. "Good day, Doctor. You know your way to the door."

eight

William didn't argue. Rising from the bench, he bid them both a courteous "Good day," then strode to the exit, his shoulders erect and his head held high.

The longing look he cast toward Lavonia just before he reached the parlor door told her she would see him again. Yet upon seeing him leave, she felt a sudden pull in her heart.

Helen cast his departing figure a withering stare as the front door shut with a thud. "Good day, indeed. I should say, *Allez-vous-en!*"

"He will not go away no matter how much you ask," Lavonia told her, "or whether the language be French or English."

"Is that so?" Helen waved her fan in front of her face with rapid motions, despite the spring chill that clung to the room.

"Why are you so vexed, Helen? I should think you would want me to find a suitor here, since you told me yourself that you think me ill suited for pioneer life in America." She watched Helen's fan move back and forth as her face took on a most disagreeable expression. A sudden thought occurred to Lavonia. "Why, Helen! If I did not know better, I would think you were jealous!"

"*Jaloux! Mais non, ma cherie!* I am concerned only for you."

Lavonia wasn't convinced. "Concerned for me? But why?"

Walking toward the bench, Helen made a motion to sit beside Lavonia. Then, cringing as though she didn't wish to occupy the place just vacated by Dr. Amory, she positioned herself instead upon the nearby sofa. Crossing her legs, she cupped her hands over her upper knee. Her fan, held by a red ribbon, dangled from the little finger of her right hand. "Our doctor has been well acquainted with many women. An innocent such as yourself is easy prey."

"I am not entirely without knowledge of the world." As soon as she blurted her defense, Lavonia wished she could take back her words.

"Then you are prepared for the wiles of Dr. Amory?" Lifting her chin, Helen looked down her nose at Lavonia.

"Wiles?" Lavonia chuckled. "Can a man not read a poem to a woman without everyone thinking he's a suitor?"

"Not that type of poem."

"How do you know? Your interruption caused him to cease reading to the end."

"Perhaps," Helen agreed, though her tone wasn't conciliatory. "Nevertheless, he knows you would make him an excellent match, Lavonia."

"Whatever do you mean?"

"The doctor knows you are my cousin. And he is aware you have recently come out of full mourning for the deaths of both your parents. Perhaps he has guessed you will be inheriting a large fortune. And now that his benefactor has expired, certainly he could make good use of the money."

"So you believe he is pursuing me for my money?"

"I do not mean to be hurtful, Lavonia. And I do hope I am wrong about his wanting you for your fortune. You have so much to offer. Your wit, your beauty, just to name two. Any man would be lucky to make a match with you. If marrying you at least in part because of your fortune is the doctor's plan, he would be most opportunistic indeed." Helen let out a sigh. "But what can one expect of someone of unknown lineage?"

"I fail to see your point."

Helen looked at her as if she had taken leave of her senses. "Why, he has a benefactor. Does that not tell you anything?"

Lavonia thought for a moment. "And what disgrace is that?

Helen, one of Father's missions was to help parentless children. He used his connections to find homes for many orphans."

"And what was his reward?" she asked.

"The joy he brought to many childless couples was reward enough on this earth, although I have no doubt he shall be awarded a jewel on his heavenly crown for each person he assisted," Lavonia answered. "My, but he must have many jewels! Who knows how many people he helped? Why, I recall a time when a young man who wanted to attend Cambridge stopped by, asking Father if he could assist with his tuition. When Father discovered he wished to pursue the ministry, he agreed to help."

"My dear uncle must have enjoyed great respect as a result."

"*Au contraire.* When he discovered I overheard the conversation, he was so embarrassed, he ordered me not to tell a soul. When I asked why, he reminded me that Jesus said that in matters of charity, 'let not your right hand know what your left is doing.' I kept my promise and did not tell a soul until this moment. And though I witnessed that act of generosity by happenstance, I suspect there were many others. As you know, he was an educated man. He wanted knowledge to be used to help others."

"If your father were here today, I wonder what he would say about William, about whether his benefactor made a good choice in helping him."

"Father put his trust in the Lord to decide whom to help. Anyone he chose would, of course, have stellar qualities."

"No doubt. But he was not *William's* benefactor." She gave Lavonia a meaningful look. "I would be reticent to rush into a betrothal with Dr. Amory."

"But no one has said he plans to marry me. No betrothal, or even courtship, was mentioned by either of us."

"Perhaps not aloud." Helen's right eyebrow arched, her way of showing disapproval. "But are you not the least bit anxious about his uncertain parentage?"

Had Helen not been serious, Lavonia would have found her concern amusing. Her own father, by his example of respect for people of all stations and classes, had taught her to place little value or emphasis on parentage. She hadn't appreciated his unique outlook until she became an adult, and society began imposing its expectations upon her. Recalling the world's bankrupt values, Lavonia cringed.

She knew Helen expected her to be shocked. In fact, Helen probably wanted her to denounce the doctor as a fraud and a cad. Weeping, followed by a delicate intake of breath before falling to the floor unconscious, would have been a performance sure to please and delight her cousin. Unwilling to give in to Helen's expectation, Lavonia stalled.

"Uncertain parentage? Whatever do you mean?"

Helen leaned toward her. "He grew up in an orphanage. According to all accounts, when William was but a month old, he was left on their doorstep one morning."

The vision brought a heaviness to her heart. She clasped her hands to her chest. "Only a month old? How sad."

"They were never told anything about him. Not why he was left there. Nothing." Sitting straight, she stretched her arms out to the sides and shrugged.

"Not even his name?"

"No. And I suppose he would have lived in obscurity had it not been for his benefactor."

"Philemon Midas."

"*Oui.*" Helen looked surprised. "But how did you know his name?"

"Dr. Amory asked me if I might know him since he was from Dover."

"Did you?"

"I am afraid not. But God must have been keeping William in his care to send a benefactor." Lavonia sighed. "Obviously his parents were in the direst of circumstances to abandon him." She imagined Dr. Amory as a baby. She wondered how anyone could resist a bright-eyed babe with a mop of dark curls and rosy cheeks, cooing in his crib.

Helen broke into her fantasy. "Obviously."

Lavonia couldn't resist a barb. "I notice the doctor's background seems to matter little when someone becomes ill."

"Of course we patronize such a fine doctor. But that does not mean he is welcome as a suitor for you, Lavonia."

She crossed her arms over her chest. "Am I not to choose my own suitors?"

"Of course you have a say," Helen assured her. "But while you remain under our roof, naturally my darling Luke shall take responsibility for you in these matters. After all, we have a duty to our family to be certain you do not make a poor match."

Lavonia clenched her teeth to prevent herself from lashing out at Helen. She knew her cousin was following the rules she had lived by all her life, and that she had Lavonia's best interests in mind. Lavonia was also aware that no amount of debate would change Helen's mind. She decided to take a different tact. "Please do not fault the doctor for circumstances well beyond his control. Surely his parents left him at the orphanage because they were desperate. Or perhaps his mother was alone, and loved her son enough to leave him where she knew he would be cared for beyond her ability to do so. Since we do not know, is it not our duty to God to give her the benefit of the doubt? Mercy, not judgment, should be our way of expressing Christian charity."

"To a woman who obviously had no morals?"

" 'Judge not, that ye be not judged.' "

" 'Condemn not, and ye shall not be condemned: forgive, and ye shall be forgiven.' " Helen continued, "Is that not Luke 6:37?"

"Oui. Tres bien."

"Merci." Helen tilted her chin upward in a prideful motion. "So you see, Lavonia, though you aspire to be a missionary overseas, you are not the only one in this family who can quote the Bible. I have attended my share of church services, too." Satisfied she had proven her point, Helen continued, "I hope you understand that I do not mean to appear harsh. You fail to realize that someone must act as judge on your behalf. You apparently are not able to see the circumstances with a sensible mind. Why, if I did not know you better, I would think you had taken leave of your senses!"

Lavonia was about to retort when the vicar's voice bellowed from the foyer. "Good morning!"

Helen gave her a look to indicate they would resume their discussion later. Lavonia dreaded when that time might arrive. She was loathe to contemplate Helen's observations. *What if Helen is right? What if the doctor is only interested in me because he believes I possess wealth?* In a flash, she recognized that her thoughts betrayed her growing affections for the man. She forced her mind onto a new path. *It matters not what the doctor thinks of me. I have no plans to marry. Not today, not tomorrow, not ever!*

Vicar Gladstone's voice broke into her troubled musings. "I could not help but overhear you, ladies. Am I to understand that you have a sister who is ill with headaches and now you have taken leave of your senses, Miss Penn?" The smirk on his face indicated a most unpleasant sort of amusement.

Not wanting the vicar to be privy to the details of their disagreement, Lavonia cast her cousin a pleading look.

Helen gave the vicar a sweet smile. "What brings you here, Vicar, so very long before the noon meal?"

If Vicar Gladstone realized Helen's implication, he didn't let his expression show it. "I am pleased to find both of you ladies well today. However, I would also care to inquire after the health of Miss Katherine Penn. I passed the doctor on my way here. Has he called on her today?"

Both women nodded.

"I am sure he is offering the finest medical treatment." The vicar's tone indicated he did not believe his own observation.

"Vraiment," Helen said. "In fact, we were just discussing what a fine doctor he is." She shot Lavonia a meaningful look.

"A better doctor than he is a Christian, I hope." Vicar Gladstone muttered the words as though he did not intend for them to be overheard, yet the volume of his voice indicated he sought comment.

Though Lavonia chose to ignore him, Helen jumped at the opportunity for an inquisition. "What causes you to make such a statement, Vicar?"

"Perhaps I should not be so free with my judgment." His look of chagrin seemed false.

"Au contraire, perhaps you should," Helen encouraged him. "After all, he is treating my dear cousin Katherine for her headaches." Her eyes flitted in Lavonia's direction. "And he has been putting romantic notions in Lavonia's head."

"Helen has always possessed a flair for fantasy," Lavonia observed.

The vicar took a seat in a wingbacked chair. "Is it a fantasy that the doctor is well acquainted with your Uncle Joseph?"

A sudden feeling of discomfiture possessed Lavonia. "I believe they may be acquaintances. I do not know the nature of their relationship or if they have any relationship at all, for that matter."

"I see." The vicar pulled on his vest in a nervous motion. "Realizing I am speaking of your family relation, I do not know how to say what I wish to impart delicately. I do not wish to give offense."

Obviously seeing she had an ally in the vicar, Helen summoned her formidable charm. "My dear Vicar. You possess much too much *savoir-faire* to give offense in your speech."

He flashed her a yellow-toothed smile. "*Oui*, but I would dearly regret *le faux-filet*."

Not expecting even the vicar to make such an egregious error in his French, Lavonia burst into laughter before she could restrain herself. Catching a glimpse of Helen, she saw that she, too, was amused. Only the vicar had taken on a peevish demeanor, indicating he had no idea he had just said he would dearly regret "sirloin."

Lavonia composed herself. "I beg your pardon, Vicar. I could not help but find your little joke amusing."

"*Oui*," agreed Helen. "How witty to substitute *faux-filet* for *faux pas*."

The vicar hesitated for an instant before a sheepish smile swept over his face. "Oh, yes, I do try to be amusing. I am of the opinion that learned clergymen such as myself have no cause to be dour. Except when the occasion requires, of course." He let out a practiced laugh.

"Your levity is appreciated," Helen said. "But we must turn to serious matters. You are among friends here. It is your duty to honor that friendship by telling us what you know about Dr. Amory and any connection he might have to our dear uncle."

"That is just the point. I have no substantive evidence about Mr. Penn and his financial dealings. Only the suspicions of many acquaintances, expressed to me in confidence, of course. But since they are all of good breeding and recognized as upstanding members of the community and the parish, I can only rely on my instinct and believe what they say."

An unpleasant twinge shot through Lavonia's midriff. She had a feeling his intuition about her uncle was correct. "Was Dr. Amory one who confided in you?"

"No. But those who do, tell me that your uncle is known for making sly investments and manipulating his dealings so that the balance is always in his favor." The vicar sighed. "To say any more would bring me treacherously close to breaking their confidence."

As far as Lavonia was concerned, he didn't need to say more. Though she neither liked nor trusted Osmond Gladstone, she knew deep down he spoke the truth. Uncle Joseph's attitude each time he had discussed estate business with her only confirmed what the vicar speculated. Her heart felt as though it had hit the bottom of her stomach. Deep in thought, she did not listen to the vicar's speech until he mentioned a name that had become increasingly dear to her.

"Dr. Amory may be as honest as any man God placed upon this great earth," he was saying. "However, if he is an associate of Mr. Penn's, then I am afraid that allowing him to become a suitor to you, Miss Penn, would be most impolitic. I even wonder at the wisdom of allowing him to come into contact with your sister at all. It would be grievous to me for her to become endangered by him in any way."

At least the vicar has lost interest in pursuing me. Now I may need to shield my dear Kitty from his clutches. . . .

"What you have told us has been most informative, Vicar," Helen said. "We shall certainly weigh your words carefully when deciding how to pursue any further relationship, if any, with the doctor."

"I hope you will, as I will not be here for at least a fortnight to render further advice. I must go to London to visit with several influential clergymen of my acquaintance." His voice was heavy with pride.

"Oh, my!" Helen clucked to show she was impressed. "I am sure your business must be of the utmost urgency to take you away for so long."

"Indeed it is. Regrettably, an older clergyman is recently deceased. It is my hope I shall be found suitable to replace him." He leaned toward Helen as if sharing a confidence.

"The new parish is quite prestigious, serving a number of London's wealthiest families."

"I am certain you will be appointed," Helen assured him. "Although if you are, we shall most assuredly be at a loss here."

"I shall miss all of you terribly, even over this fortnight. Thankfully, Vicar Weems has agreed to conduct services here in my absence."

Lavonia nodded. On both occasions she had met Vicar Weems, he had impressed her as a man of God.

"I do wonder if Katherine will even notice my absence."

"Undoubtedly." Always one to make a match, Helen arose from her seat. "In fact, she is sewing in the drawing room at this very moment. Shall I escort you?"

"Please."

Lavonia tarried as they left. Looking out of the picture window, she watched the heavy rainfall water the expansive lawn. She had been detained so long that the church meeting was sure to be over. She sighed. "Perhaps it is just as well. I feel as gray as the sky."

"Are you coming, Lavonia?" Helen asked, sticking her head back into the room.

"All right, Helen." She had no desire to watch her sister become enchanted with the vicar. But perhaps that was better than sitting alone, nursing renewed doubts about William Amory.

nine

"Oh, dear Vonnie, please do not force me to go to Aunt Amelia's!" Katherine collapsed into several down pillows situated on her bed, to which she had retired after being revived with smelling salts.

"I am pleased to see you are well enough to complain."

Katherine grimaced. "I must speak despite my illness, lest I be shipped off to Aunt Amelia's as I sleep!" Retaining her prone position, she folded her arms over her chest in an act of defiance.

Lavonia patted her hand. "Perhaps we should await Dr. Amory's diagnosis before making any decisions."

"Will he be here soon?"

"Helen sent word that he was to come immediately." Lavonia gave her a shamefaced look. "Although I feel rather foolish now that I see you merely fainted."

"*Au contraire,* Vonnie. My fainting might not be trivial at all. This incident could simply be a precursor of worse evils to come!" Demonstrating her usual flair for drama, Katherine reached for the smelling salts on the nightstand beside her bed. Uncorking the small bottle made of clear glass, she took a dainty whiff. Her eyes opened wide as the pungent odor hit her nose. Shaking her head, she looked revitalized as she closed the bottle and returned it to its place beside her bed.

"You seem to be feeling better already. Almost like your old self," Lavonia observed.

"But not well enough to make the trip to London." She began to sniffle. "Vonnie, could you please hand me a kerchief out of my vanity drawer?"

Nodding, Lavonia set to do her sister's bidding. "You must be terribly disappointed. Aunt Amelia's letters about life in the city always seemed to brighten your days."

"Yes, but perhaps life in London is not all I thought it might be."

Lavonia patted her sister's hand. "Perhaps not. But Aunt Amelia is certain to be vexed if she has traveled all this way just to find you plan to stay here after all."

"I know. And I do hate to disappoint her." Katherine looked at Lavonia with misty eyes. One by one, tears fell on her cheeks. After taking the kerchief from Lavonia, she patted each cheek dry. "But she can find someone else to live with her, *oui?*"

"Perhaps. But you have always been her favorite niece."

Her features brightening at the flattery, Katherine let her hands, still holding the kerchief, drop to her lap. "Yes, I always have been." A triumphant smile crossed her lips. "But of course, she simply adores you and Helen, too."

"Whatever you say." Not looking at her sister, Lavonia bent over the bed and smoothed the covers.

Katherine sniffled into her kerchief. "You will tell Aunt Amelia how disappointed I am that I cannot go back with her?"

"In due time. But I shall delay."

A stricken look crossed Katherine's face. *"Pourquoi?"*

"Because, my dear sister, I am hoping that as the days pass, you will find yourself well enough to go to London with her after all. As you recall," Lavonia said, pulling the covers over Katherine's chest with one final pat, "she plans to stay a full fortnight."

"Is that all? Really, a fortnight is hardly enough time for me to recover. No, she will have to go back to London"—pausing, she let out a sigh—"without me."

"But if you cannot go to London, where will you go, Dearest?"

"Could I not remain here?" Katherine looked about the

darkened room. An expression filled with fondness crossed her features, as if she had lived in the room since childhood. Katherine let out a dramatic breath. "Helen is so kind."

"I agree. But we have imposed upon her hospitality quite enough." Bringing herself to her full height, Lavonia placed her hands on her hips. "If you do not wish to go to London, then you shall go to America with me."

Kitty bolted upright. "Go and live in America!" She nearly spat out the country's name. "*Mais non!* I would never do such a thing!"

"And why not? We have lived together in the same house ever since you were born."

"Oh, Vonnie, I would rather be with you than anyone else in the world. It is just that. . ." Kitty stopped herself. Widening her eyes and softening her lips, she gave Lavonia a soulful look. "Please, will you stay here, Vonnie?"

Lavonia braced herself against her sister's pleading. "There is nothing here for me," she managed to say with enough assurance that she believed it herself.

"*Au contraire,* there is much for you here. Helen adores you, and so do I." She raised an eyebrow as if she dared Lavonia to argue. "And so does the doctor."

Before Lavonia could answer, Helen breezed into the room. "But of course I adore you, Lavonia. You have always been special to me." Helen rolled her eyes toward the door to indicate she wasn't alone. "Dr. Amory is here to see Katherine."

At the mention of the doctor's name, Lavonia's heart felt as though it would jump high enough to land in her throat. *How much did he overhear?*

Dr. Amory strode into the room. "I beg your pardon for taking so long. I arrived as soon as I could."

"That is quite all right," Lavonia murmured. Against her will, she averted her eyes from his handsome face.

"I would have been here sooner, but I was in the midst of

painting at the Roths'. I had to return to my room to retrieve my medical bag before I could come."

His crisp voice gave Lavonia the courage to look into his face. In his eyes she saw not the condemnation mixed with amusement she had feared, but genuine concern for Katherine. She hoped his demeanor meant that he had no plans to inquire into whatever he had overheard.

"How regrettable that your work was interrupted," Helen observed.

"The Roths were understanding. They know medical emergencies take precedence over their portraits."

"Of course they do," Kitty agreed.

He cut his gaze to Katherine. "And how are you by now, Miss Penn?"

"I am so glad to see you, Doctor. I am feeling quite poorly after my attack."

"Yes, your spell was quite sudden. Has this ever happened before?"

"No."

He looked surprised. "What do you think caused it?"

Katherine's eyes widened. "I really do not know, Doctor. The whole incident is a mystery to me."

"Were you exerting yourself at the time?"

Katherine shook her head. "No. I was having tea. And listening to Aunt Amelia."

"And you get on well with your aunt?"

"Oh yes!" Katherine lifted her chin proudly. "Everyone says I am her favorite niece. Is that not right?" She looked to the two women.

"Oui, oui!" Helen agreed before she was interrupted by Luke's entrance.

"May I see you a moment, *ma femme belle?*"

"Mais oui, le mari!" Helen answered, her face beaming as it always did whenever Luke referred to her as his beautiful

wife. She turned to the others. *"Excusez-moi, s'il vous plaît."*

As William watched them exit, Lavonia couldn't help but notice that he seemed pleased to be rid of Helen. He turned to Lavonia. "Now, where were we?"

"We were conferring about the event surrounding Katherine's fainting spell," Lavonia reminded him. "When my sister collapsed, Aunt Amelia was in the midst of discussing the work Katherine would do once she takes up residence with her in London."

She thought she saw a hint of a smile touch his lips before he straightened his mouth into a serious line. "Oh? What type of work?"

Katherine wrinkled her nose. "She wants me to do housework."

Tilting his chin, Dr. Amory rubbed it with the thumb and forefinger of his right hand. "From what little I know of you, Miss Penn, I surmise you are unaccustomed to heavy work?"

"Oui!" She flashed him a sweet smile. "Aunt Amelia did not actually say I would be expected to do such awful work. She was simply telling us that we will temporarily be short one maid, that is all. And of course, I told her I could certainly make do until we find someone to take her place." Rolling her eyes skyward, Katherine clasped her hands to her chest and let out a tortured breath. "I would like to help my dear aunt. Really, I would. But I am simply too sick to do the maid's chores. Oh, how awful it is to be ill!"

"Indeed." The doctor nodded. "I notice your cheeks are not flushed, as they generally are when you have a fever."

"Are you quite sure? I do feel oh, so hot." Withdrawing a fan from a drawer of her nightstand, she began cooling her face with rapid motions.

"I have not seen you demonstrate any other symptoms since I arrived."

As if on cue, Katherine began to hack. "Oh, I do beg your

pardon!" she apologized after several coughs. "Dr. Amory, I despise that you must see me like this. I know my illness causes me to appear most unladylike."

"That is quite all right. Illness knows not of etiquette."

With a quick motion, Katherine threw her hand onto her head. "Oh no! I seem to have developed a headache as well. Oh, why must I suffer so?"

"Why, indeed?" Dr. Amory seemed more amused than concerned. "Miss Penn, I recommend you continue to rest until you feel better." He turned to exit.

"But, Dr. Amory," Katherine protested, "you have barely examined me at all."

Stopping in his pace, he returned his gaze to his patient. "I believe you are overtired. Plenty of rest should take care of that."

Deflated, Katherine turned over in her bed and nestled into the down pillows.

Crooking his forefinger, he motioned for Lavonia to join him in the hall. Without words, he led her down the stairs and into the parlor.

Lavonia couldn't contain herself once her feet passed the threshold. "I surmise you did not wish to alarm my sister, Doctor. But please, be frank with me. Is she very ill?"

"What is your opinion, Miss Penn?"

Lavonia was taken aback by his question. "My opinion? Why, I have not formed an opinion. I defer to your knowledge for a diagnosis, Dr. Amory."

"All right. I shall give you my opinion." He took in a breath as though he were summoning his courage. "First of all, I believe your sister's symptoms are real."

"Of course they are."

He lifted his forefinger. "Please, allow me to finish. I believe they are real, but I have noticed a pattern. Have you not seen it as well?"

Lavonia thought for a moment. "Her illnesses do take on the pattern you described earlier in that she seems sicker at some times than at others. You said the degree is related to her happiness, but no other doctor has made such an observation."

"Then let me ask you. How was your sister's health before the arrival of your aunt?"

"For the past few days, her health has been nearly perfect."

He nodded. "I suspected as much. Now, am I to understand that she fainted while your aunt was discussing the prospect of Katherine taking on the duties of the maid?"

"Yes."

"And she was taken by surprise by your aunt's request?"

"Yes. I was taken by surprise as well. I had no idea Katherine would be expected to labor so." Her mouth curved. "You see, Dr. Amory, she was sheltered from hard work by my parents when they were alive, and I try not to expose her to too much effort now. So frankly, I can see why she fainted at the prospect of such a change."

"Would you?" The doctor let out a laugh.

"I fail to see what amuses you, Dr. Amory." Her chilly tone belied her indignation as she noticed how the sun drifting through the picture window highlighted his deep eyes. The rays created shadows accentuating his straight nose and crafted face. His laugh was more melodic than the most enchanting song. How could she find the one who was mocking her, and her sister, so charming? Bracing herself, she set about making her voice ominous. "Do you not realize how delicate my sister is? Such physical work could place her in grave danger!"

"Do you really believe that?"

She was taken aback by his challenge. "Why, why. . .of course!"

"Then you are either lying to yourself or you are a fool."

"A fool! How dare you!" The tone of her voice was no less

sharp than as if she had slapped him across the cheek.

"I beg your pardon. Perhaps I should not be so blunt." His eyes shone with regret. "Let us discuss this another time, when neither of us is vexed."

"There shall be no other time, Dr. Amory." Anger welling inside her, Lavonia blurted, "I have no objection to scrubbing floors. I shall go live with Aunt Amelia, and take Katherine with me. You need not worry about either of us again."

ten

"But I do worry about you," William objected.

"Why?" Though she was filled with rage, she noticed that he seemed calm. Suddenly she felt ashamed at herself for her outburst, when all he seemed to harbor for her was compassion.

She wanted to keep her voice crisp, but her soft tone betrayed her conflicting emotions. "Why do you worry about me? I can take care of myself."

"Can you?" He seemed to be seeking an answer rather than offering a retort. "But I thought Christians rely upon the Lord."

The truth of his observation fueled her vexation. "I have no desire to debate with you, Doctor."

"And I do not wish to debate with you." Placing a strong hand on each of her shoulders, his lips parted as his eyes searched her face. Her heart racing, Lavonia froze, unsure whether he planned to kiss her or to speak. After hesitating, he chose the latter.

"If you want to leave, that is fine with me. I have nothing to say about it." He let go of her as if to confirm his statement.

Lavonia's heart sank at his words. *So he cares not for me after all?*

"But first, I ask that you favor me by granting one request.

Her curiosity got the better of her. "What?"

"Go with me to the Stone place at two in the afternoon on Sunday."

The Stone family were farmers with a brood of children ranging in age from infancy to teens. She remembered that on his previous visit with Katherine, the doctor was planning to see their sick baby on his way home. "How is the baby?"

"So you remembered." A smile of pleasure was her reward. "Little Isaac just has a touch of colic."

"Poor little thing. I hope it shall pass soon."

"The goat's milk should start to help in a few days. Until then, I suppose his crying causes his parents more trouble in sleepless nights than anything else."

Lavonia couldn't help but notice how his face glowed when he spoke about his patients. Even when other doctors would have been at wit's end with Katherine, William always tempered firmness with a strong dose of kindness. "What a blessing you are."

He gave her a quizzical look. "What was that you just whispered?"

Surprised that she had uttered her thought aloud, Lavonia answered, "Nothing. It was nothing."

Though his expression indicated he didn't quite believe her, he gallantly changed the subject. "So will you go with me?"

"If you will tell me what business I could possibly have with the Stones."

"You shall know when we get there."

"Do you think it proper for a lady to go to a strange place with a man, unescorted?"

"If you fear traveling two miles in a carriage with me, Miss Penn, I surmise you will survive less than a week in pioneer country." His violet eyes held a dare, mixed with amusement.

Too proud not to accept his challenge, Lavonia willingly fell into his trap. "Very well. I shall go with you. But mind you, there had better be good reason."

"I shall leave it to you to decide that, Miss Penn." He tipped his hat, his eyes twinkling with mischief. "Good day."

 махов

"I simply will not allow you to go." Helen stood by Lavonia's bed, watching her sort clothing in preparation for her trip to

London. Folding her hands in a gesture of defiance, she brought herself up to her full height. With a definite clack of each heel, she positioned her feet on the floor.

Despite Helen's fortitude, Lavonia folded a few garments. Though she wasn't ready to leave, either physically or mentally, packing her belongings would show Helen she was serious about her imminent departure. "But I must. The time has come."

"I beg to differ," Helen persisted. "Surely you do not wish to live with Aunt Amelia. She will make you nothing more than a common servant."

Turning from her task, Lavonia caught Helen's gaze. "I am already a servant of the Lord's. If His plan for me is to help Aunt Amelia, then I am to obey His will."

"No doubt your laboring for Aunt Amelia is her will." Helen tilted her chin upward. "I fail to see why you seem to prefer her company to mine."

Exasperated by Helen's conclusion, her chest heaved with a heavy breath. "You know that is not true. But Katherine and I have imposed on your kind hospitality long enough."

"Why have you decided so suddenly upon this new arrangement?"

"I know my decision seems abrupt to you. But I have been considering it for a long time."

Helen's right eyebrow rose. "Why do I think this decision of yours has something to do with Dr. Amory?"

Lavonia stopped folding midstream, a coarse woolen muffler in her hand. She wanted to protest, but couldn't bring herself to deny Helen's observation. She swallowed before trying to steady her voice. "Dr. Amory? What makes you think that?"

Helen chuckled, placing her hands on her slim hips. "Do you think everyone in this house is blind? Of course we have seen the way you look at each other. You are hopelessly in love with the doctor. Why will you not admit it?"

"Admit it? There is nothing to admit." At that moment a shadow obscured the light from the hall. Glancing in that direction, Lavonia was relieved to see a figure in white perched in the doorway. "What are you doing out of bed, Kitty?"

Her sister floated toward her. "As terrible as I feel, I just had to see you. Please tell me what I heard is not true, Vonnie."

So Helen has told Kitty we are leaving! Lavonia shot Helen a withering look.

Helen raised her hands in mock protest. "I did not tell her, Lavonia."

"That is correct. Aunt Amelia told me we are leaving."

Lavonia's gaze fired in Helen's direction. "Then you told Aunt Amelia our plans, Helen."

Though Helen shrugged, her voice grew high-pitched as she defended herself. "She had to know! After all, she is the one who will be most affected by the change in circumstance."

Lavonia threw the muffler on the bed in a vain attempt to vent her anger. "I wanted to be the one to tell Aunt Amelia that I'll be coming, too. In fact, I *should* have been the one to tell her, not you."

Helen's mouth twisted, but she remained silent rather than issuing the apology Lavonia expected.

"It matters not who told whom what," Katherine pointed out. "Are we really going to London, Vonnie? If we are, I want to hear the truth from your lips."

"Yes, we are."

"I would not be so sure of that. I understand from Aunt Amelia that you never asked her permission?"

"Not yet, but—"

Unannounced, Aunt Amelia breezed into the room. "No, she certainly has not asked me." She gave Lavonia a chastising look. "One would think you would have remembered your manners, Lavonia, and asked before inviting yourself to live with me."

Lavonia was taken aback by her aunt's accusation. "But I thought—"

"You thought nothing of whether or not I can afford to take on not one, but two impoverished nieces."

Stung by the truth, Lavonia swallowed. "But I can—"

"Earn your keep?" Aunt Amelia let out a decisive sniff. "I need not but one maid, and I doubt if you can cook as well as the woman currently in my employ."

Aunt Amelia's objections left Lavonia feeling helpless. Never had she suspected her aunt would turn her away. She blurted out the first solution that popped into her head. "London is a big city. Certainly, there would be a job there for an able-bodied woman."

Katherine let out a laugh. "You may be able-bodied, but you have never done any serious work in your life."

"I can sew."

"You can mend, certainly," Katherine said. "But we have always employed a dressmaker."

"I can learn to sew. And I hear one can make a good wage remaking dresses." She nodded to her sister. "Refashioning old garments is a skill with which both of us will soon become well acquainted, I am sure."

"A woman of your station might be better suited to the work of a nanny or governess," Aunt Amelia suggested.

Her counsel gave Lavonia hope. "Certainly. Why, I was planning to do such work for Jane, in any event."

"Then why not pursue that?" Aunt Amelia asked.

Lavonia shook her head. "She is unable to pay me. And since I must support both Katherine and myself, I am afraid I must take paid employment." She cast her aunt a pleading look. "Could you let me stay with you, just until I find work? Then Katherine and I could both move out."

"Oh, to have a family member reduced to such!" Helen wailed.

"I agree," Katherine said. "Only the poor and destitute, with nowhere else to turn, should have to be reduced to common work."

"I am not ashamed to do honest work. One's station is a poor substitute for leg of mutton to fill one's stomach and coal to keep one's feet warm." Lavonia sighed. "I confess, working in London was not my plan. But as I told Helen, perhaps it is God's intention for me."

"How can you say that about a loving God?" asked Katherine. "Why would He let you sink so low, when you say you are His servant?"

"Know you nothing about the life of Jesus?" Lavonia challenged her. "God never promised a life of luxury and ease for His servants. Even His own Son lived well below what should have been his place in the world."

Chastened, Katherine remained silent, but Aunt Amelia was not so shy. "I must beg to differ. God sent Jesus as an example to us. But that does not mean we should suffer!" A huff escaped her lips. "My dearly departed father did not earn his fortune so I would be forced to live like a common house maid. Before Joseph became my financial manager, my hands were never dirty. I ate the finest food money could buy. I had so many friends, my house was full of merriment both day and night. But now, all of that is gone. I have not had a new dress made in two years. I eat pea soup for supper." Her eyes roved over Lavonia and Kitty. "And I look for help among my nieces, and I am weary of labor I was never meant to do."

"Weary, already?" Katherine asked. "But I thought your maid just left."

"Whatever gave you such a notion? Why, she has been gone for over a year."

Lavonia saw Katherine's and Helen's mouths drop open in shock. Uneasiness caused her own stomach to roil. Oblivious to the fact she had revealed her own deceit, their aunt continued, "Her departure was fortuitous, in reality. I was planning to fire her in any event, to save money."

"So you never planned to hire anyone else," Katherine's observation was spoken softly, a revelation to herself that required no response.

"I know your plight seems grim," Lavonia said to her aunt, "but certainly there are people in worse circumstances."

"The concerns of the heathen poor matter little to me. I am not like them." She tilted her chin in a prideful manner. "I have been on the membership roster at church for over fifty years."

Helen interjected, "Everyone knows you are a good person, Aunt Amelia."

"Then why did God let me lose my fortune?" Her eyes widened in puzzlement.

After pausing for a moment of contemplation, Helen bowed her head. "I wish I knew."

Aunt Amelia's eyes bored into Lavonia. "What about you? Surely you can offer me an answer."

"I can offer you only Scripture, our Lord's inspired Word." Though she didn't have an instant to pray, The Holy Spirit answered her unspoken cry. "Do you remember the parable in the twelfth chapter of Luke about the rich man who built more and more barns to store all his goods?"

"Yes. So he could retire." Aunt Amelia's voice became enthusiastic. "How I would love to rest, and not burden this weary body any more!" Her gaze passed over the blank faces of three young women. "You will know one day, what it is like to be old and tired."

"If that is the Lord's will," Lavonia added. "But the Bible does not promise anyone a long life, as that parable shows. 'But God said unto him, Thou fool, this night thy soul shall be required of thee: then whose shall those things be, which thou hast provided? So is he that layeth up treasure for himself, and is not rich toward God.' "

The words were barely uttered before their aunt responded. "I have always given money to the church, and what was my thanks? To lose my fortune. And if that were not enough, He's taken my youth and energy along with it."

"But, Auntie," Katherine protested. "You are still ever so popular! Why, think of the last letter you wrote to us. All the feasts, dancing, and parties—"

"The feasts give me indigestion, the dancing gives me sore feet, and the parties run too far into the night for me to get a decent night's rest," she complained. "The world is for the young and rich. I am no longer either."

"So use this time to draw closer to the Lord," suggested Lavonia.

"When He has taken everything from me? No. God abandoned me, because He did not care for me. I see no need to warm the church pew." Satisfied that she had made her point, Aunt Amelia lifted her nose into the air.

"He has not abandoned you," Lavonia argued.

Aunt Amelia didn't flinch. "What do you know of life? You are still a babe."

"Perhaps. But I can pray for you."

Her face hardened into a disagreeable pose. "I do not request your prayers."

"But you cannot stop me from praying for you."

Her aunt looked angry. "Do not waste your time."

"My time is the Lord's. I shall pray as I feel His calling." Already Lavonia knew her first prayer would be for her aunt to understand Him.

ॐ

"There you are," Lavonia said to her sister the following day upon finding her in the kitchen. Katherine was wearing her oldest housedress underneath an apron that had seen better days. "Whatever are you doing?"

"Betsy said she would teach me how to make beeswax candles."

Lavonia thought about the feisty bees Luke kept. They provided the household with delicious honey, although sometimes at a price. "Be careful not to get stung."

"Oh, she has already collected the wax." Katherine chuckled. "I just hope Betsy keeps the soap-making chores to herself." Katherine grimaced. Extending her soft, unlined hands, she gave them a loving look and sighed. "I am loathe to possess the hands of a common scrub woman."

"No matter what work you face, rubbing a little chicken grease each day will keep them smooth."

"So my hands can smell as bad as they look, I suppose." Katherine wrinkled her nose. Letting out a resolute sigh, she dropped her hands to her side. "So why were you looking for me?"

"I was wondering if you have seen my writing paper. I must inform Jane that I will not be coming to America, after all." Though Lavonia tried to conceal her disappointment, she knew her voice betrayed her.

"Your writing paper?" Kitty gave her a sheepish look. "I used the last bit of it for a letter."

Lavonia raised an eyebrow. "A letter? To whom?"

"Vicar Gladstone."

Lavonia lifted her arms in an exasperated motion. "If you really had to use my paper, I wish it could have been for better purpose."

Katherine chose to ignore her sister's complaint. "Surely Helen has some you can use."

"An excellent suggestion. Do you know where she is?"

"She and Luke are out with the horses."

Lavonia looked at the small clock positioned on the table near the fireplace. "It is early yet. I suppose they shall be gone a bit longer."

Katherine shrugged. "Write it later."

"No. I have been putting off this letter for too long. Surely Helen will not mind if I borrow a sheet of her writing paper."

Lavonia strode briskly up the stairs to the study situated opposite one of the guest bedchambers. The heavy oak door let out a protesting creak as she entered the hideaway.

The room, decorated in gold and green, was still except for the steady ticking of a grandfather clock. Shelves stocked with old textbooks, works of Shakespeare, and the flighty novels Helen enjoyed, lined the walls. The mahogany secretary Luke and Helen shared was tidy. Lavonia was confident she could find the paper she sought with ease. The top of the desk served as temporary storage for the week's unanswered correspondence, along with two periodicals and the day's newspaper.

Seeing no writing paper, she opened the largest drawer, just beneath the desk top. Clucking her tongue in disappointment when writing paper did not make itself readily apparent, she rifled through a stack of stored papers, trying to disturb them as little as possible in hopes of finding the writing paper she sought at the bottom of the pile.

Her search had not ended when she spotted a name that caught her attention. "Philemon Midas." She paused to think. *Where have I heard that name?* A sudden realization met her. *Philemon Midas! Why, he's William's benefactor.*

Curiosity overcoming her, Lavonia extracted the document from the rest of the papers. "Deed of sale," she read. Scanning the deed, Lavonia discovered it was the paperwork for the sale of her own house in Dover. To her shock, the price paid for the house was ten thousand pounds more than her uncle had said the property brought.

That's more than enough for passage to America! How could Uncle Joseph keep that money from me? And even more puzzling, how could the house have sold to William's benefactor?

Pausing to contemplate what she had just seen, Lavonia had a startling thought.

Can it be that William's benefactor is still alive?

eleven

Lavonia wondered what she should do. For the next few moments, she fantasized about confronting Luke, and what his answer might be. Lavonia's hands were shaking as she restored the documents to their original place. Asking Luke about it would avail naught, surely. He had simply taken the papers from her uncle for safekeeping. She doubted he knew Philemon Midas, or his connection to William. And certainly Helen would know nothing.

Too distraught to write to Jane, Lavonia tiptoed out of the study, closed the door behind her, and retreated to her bedchamber. She resolved to pray for guidance. Sitting on the side of her bed, her feet dangling from its high side, she prayed. Closing her eyes in further contemplation, she found no call to action. The Lord seemed to be telling her to wait.

But I don't want to wait, Lord. Why must I wait to find the answer?

Sighing, Lavonia bowed her head. *Lord, does this mean You wish me to stay here? Or are You simply testing my faith, to see if I will remain your servant regardless of whether I have a lot or a little?*

At that moment, she felt led to open the Bible she clutched in both hands. She had heard from reliable sources that John Wesley sought answers to life's problems by opening his Bible at random, looking for the Lord's leading. She decided to do likewise.

Her Bible opened to the sixth chapter of Paul's first letter to Timothy. Starting with the fifth verse, she read:

But godliness with contentment is great gain. For we brought nothing into this world, and it is certain we can carry nothing out. And having food and raiment let us be therewith content. But they that will be rich fall into temptation and a snare, and into many foolish and hurtful lusts, which drown men in destruction and perdition. For the love of money is the root of all evil: which while some coveted after, they have erred from the faith, and pierced themselves through with many sorrows. But thou, O man of God, flee these things; and follow after righteousness, godliness, faith, love, patience, meekness.

She thought about the words, wondering if the financial loss was a test of her faith.

"But they that will be rich fall into temptation and a snare." Despite her best efforts not to pass judgment, those words brought to mind her uncle. Had her money tempted him to steal? Was she guilty for the mere possession of wealth? Had she been poor, her fortune would not have tempted her uncle.

Well, she resolved, she would have the answer, and soon. Although she wasn't sure if she was ready to face the truth.

&

"A fine day this is, indeed," William said as he guided the carriage down the country lane.

"Indeed." Lavonia breathed a whiff of spring air, scented by delicate blossoms on the trees and shrubs they passed. A light shower had given way to soft sunshine, resulting in a pale blue sky dotted with fluffy clouds. Though she wanted to ask William about his benefactor, she found herself unwilling to mar the pleasure of their journey together.

"And so much the better in the company of such a lady."

"Such a flatterer you are!" She felt her cheeks grow warm. "You should have been at worship with me this morning. The vicar preached a sermon on Proverbs."

William flashed her a teasing smile. "And what did the good vicar say?"

"He quoted Proverbs 26:28. 'A lying tongue hateth those that are afflicted by it; and a flattering mouth worketh ruin.' "

"I confess neither to flattery nor to lying." He took his eyes from the road long enough to shoot her a teasing look. "Unless you, Miss Penn, are indeed no lady."

Her mouth twisted into a chastising curl. "If I were not certain you speak in jest, I would take offense to your remark, Dr. Amory."

"I suspect you shall be in need of a sense of humor to witness for the Lord, especially in a Methodist household. What is that expression they use when the weather is foul?"

Lavonia knew the answer all too well. "There is nothing out today but crows and Methodist preachers."

"Yes, they are a hardy lot, are they not?" William chuckled.

"They must be robust to maintain their schedules. Preaching at five in the morning then again each evening, seven days a week, with travel in between, can break a noble constitution as well as one's health. But the rewards have been great. Our denomination has experienced tremendous growth in the colonies. In some parts, Methodists offer the only available religious service." Speaking about the success of Methodism gave Lavonia a surge of pride in the accomplishments of the ministers. "Our Methodist circuit riders are quite dedicated to the Lord's cause."

"Speaking of dedication to a cause, I am surprised to hear you say Vicar Gladstone preached a sermon on flattery this morning." William chuckled. "Considering his campaign for a London parish, certainly he makes good employ of artful words. I should have liked to see him preach on guile while trying to keep a serious expression!"

Lavonia joined his laughter. "Indeed, I would have enjoyed witnessing such a sermon myself. But it was not Vicar

Gladstone who preached, but Vicar Weems."

"No wonder." He gave her a knowing nod. "So you find worship at your cousin's church appealing?"

"I suppose. Though I do confess, I miss the Methodist meetings Father conducted."

William seemed surprised. "You mean to say, he was a Methodist preacher?"

"Not exactly." Lavonia hesitated. "He was a businessman by trade. But he preached as the Lord called."

"He was a lay preacher, then."

Lavonia nodded.

"What an unusual circumstance for an English business-man to espouse Methodism. Surely remaining an Anglican, as the majority of his colleagues most assuredly were, would have proven more profitable?"

"Father was not as interested in profits as he was in peo-ple, especially after he experienced his conversion." Lavonia sighed. "If only I could influence Helen. . ."

"Your cousin is a bit strong-willed," William observed, "so I would not become discouraged if I were you. Though I confess, I feared you might not go with me today, lest she should object."

Her conscience gave Lavonia a prick as she remembered how she stepped lightly out of the house without so much as a "by your leave" from Helen. "What she does not know will not harm us," Lavonia said, trying to keep her voice light.

"Indeed?" William's eyebrows arched. "I am not certain I would wish to face Mrs. Syms when she is angered."

"I shall worry about the consequences later."

When he didn't answer, Lavonia studied his profile. Dark, boyish curls peeked from under his hat, their impishness contrasting with his straight nose. William's mouth was set in a soft line, suggesting that anything the least bit funny could send him into thundering laughter. His eyes seemed to be drinking in the blue sky, so rare after a week of drizzling rain. The horse's rhythmic clopping offered a soothing sound in accompaniment to the occasional gust of breeze. After the turmoil of Aunt Amelia's visit and Katherine's bouts of illness, Lavonia found she was in no humor to break the spell of the comfortable, meditative silence.

A few moments later, nervousness swept over her as they made the turn onto the dirt road leading past strawberry fields and on to the Stones' house where a few buggies and horses were hitched in the side yard. "You did not tell me there would be other people here."

"Does that bother you?"

"No," she answered too quickly. "I only wish you would tell me why we are here."

"Has your trust in me diminished?"

She shook her head.

"Then be patient. I promise you will be pleasantly surprised."

Several people were approaching the house on foot. Most were strangers to her. But some of them, such as the local shopkeeper, had become familiar since she first arrived. Their simple modes of dress indicated most were of modest means, though a few were dressed in the finery of the wealthy. She wondered what all these people could have in common to cause them to assemble here.

The touch of William's hand, clad in kidskin gloves, took her mind off her musings as he helped her exit the carriage. His touch was all too brief, ending as soon as her feet lit upon the ground. He gave her a reassuring smile. As she smiled in return, her glance caught the Bible he carried in the crook of his arm.

"Why did you bring your Bible?"

"Do you not take your Bible to church?" he teased.

"Church? But this is not—"

He shook his head back and forth quickly, causing her to

cease her objections. Without warning, an idea materialized. *But no. It could not be.*

All was quiet when they entered the large kitchen. There were no chairs, save two occupied by elderly ladies. Had chairs been offered, space would not have permitted everyone to sit as the room filled with worshipers.

Soon after she and William arrived, the ceremony began. Lavonia easily joined in the singing of "O For A Thousand Tongues To Sing" without musical accompaniment or hymn books. The hymn, written by John Wesley's brother Charles, was already a Methodist standard. Charles had proven a prolific writer of hymns during his lifetime. Lavonia had heard he wrote at least one hymn a day, totaling somewhere between 6,000 and 8,000.

Stealing a look at William, she saw his face alight with joy as he sang without hesitation in a pleasing baritone. Though she had admired his countenance upon many occasions, he was more radiant at that moment than she had ever observed. She wondered how long he had shared her faith, and she wondered about the conversion that allowed him to accept Methodism along with the free salvation offered only through the blood of Jesus Christ.

Unlike the learned clergy of other denominations, Mr. Stone preached extemporaneously, without any papers or notes. The verse he selected was Matthew 5:29: "And if thy right eye offend thee, pluck it out, and cast it from thee: for it is profitable for thee that one of thy members should perish, and not that thy whole body should be cast into hell."

Lavonia had heard sermons on this verse on numerous occasions. Methodists were enthusiastic about ridding themselves of sin in hopes of one day achieving what John Wesley called "Christian Perfection." For over an hour, Mr. Stone admonished his congregation to purge themselves of all manner of sin or suffer consequences too dire to be contemplated by human imaginations. His warnings, delivered in a melodious cadence, were punctuated by enthusiastic gestures, pacing, and colorful facial expressions. His efforts were rewarded by shouts, crying, clapping, and confessions.

The style of worship was alien to the staid formality of the church where Lavonia and her family attended before her own conversion. There, the learned clergyman read dry sermons from prepared text. The congregation followed the service by rote, demonstrating little, if any, emotion. Lavonia relished the Methodist enthusiasm, but Katherine had been disappointed when her parents and Lavonia had pledged their allegiance to Methodism, and she had continued to worship at the Anglican church.

Lavonia's musings were interrupted by the benediction. After thanking Mr. Stone for the insights he offered in his sermon and Mrs. Stone for her hospitality, Lavonia was introduced to many of the other parishioners. Many gave her and William curious looks, as if wondering if William were her suitor. Feelings of triumph and self-satisfaction welled inside her when she noticed a few envious glances from women who wore no wedding bands.

My pride reminds me I have far to go before attaining Christian perfection.

"So, how did you like my little surprise?" William asked as they left the meeting and headed for the waiting carriage. A smug look covered his handsome features.

"Surprised I am," she admitted. "And you allowed me to chatter at length about Methodism. What a bore I must be!"

"*Au contraire,* Miss Penn. I found what you had to say quite interesting."

"But certainly you must know all about Methodism. Although I admit, I never suspected you are one of us."

"Oh?" Taking her elbow, he assisted her as she climbed into the carriage. "What faith did you think I practiced?"

Lavonia moved so he could take his place beside her on the bench. "I suppose I did not think you had much faith at all."

He looked puzzled. "Why?"

She hesitated, averting her eyes to her shoes. "Do you want the truth?"

"Yes," she heard him answer.

"All right, then." Still focusing on her shoes, she replied, "All reports of you and your past have not been favorable ones." Having delivered the blow, she cut her glance to him and saw him wince.

"What reports?"

"Are you certain you wish to know?"

"Does not everyone wish to know what is said behind their back?" Though his tone was light, she knew he was serious. She waited as he clucked his tongue against his teeth, signaling the horse to move.

Sighing, she knew it would be a long journey home.

twelve

William's stomach churned as he watched Lavonia summon the courage to speak. Her blue eyes had taken on a distressed light. Her pink lips were slightly parted, though no words escaped. Her face, the color of purest cream by nature, had turned several shades whiter. And her usual fire had been replaced by the posture of a nervous woman he didn't recognize, who was picking imaginary lint from her dress and shifting in her seat.

How much had she heard? And how will I answer the charges?

He wished he hadn't asked for the details, but he *had* to know what she had heard. Otherwise, how could he fight back? He prayed that whatever Lavonia had heard wouldn't keep her from loving him. Though he knew it would be wise to discuss the past some time during their courtship, William had hoped the bad news could wait until Lavonia had fallen for him as deeply as he had fallen for her. Perhaps that notion would not be considered fair play, but he already had obstacles enough with her cousin's objections.

Lavonia's sweet voice interrupted his anxious thoughts. "Dr. Amory—"

"Please," he blurted, "call me William."

A brief smile lit her features. Just as quickly, a look of doubt replaced it. "Are you certain such familiarity between us would be proper?"

"I would prefer it, yes." He paused. "Unless you are not comfortable—"

"Oh yes, I am." Her gaze fell to her shoes. "But I would

not want to be so forward that you begin to think I am not a lady."

William held back a chuckle. The high-spirited Miss Penn, though unmistakably a lady, bore no resemblance to the reticent, priggish maidens who took pride in being called a lady, while their stodgy demeanors kept them always at arms' length.

He pulled the carriage to the side of the road. A clearing of emerald-colored grass surrounded by dogwood trees with pink and white blooms invited them to sit and enjoy God's creation. Pausing for a moment, he let his eyes drink in the beauty of the isolated area.

Lavonia's voice interrupted his meditation. "Why did you pull over? Is something amiss?"

"Quite the contrary, Miss Penn. I have yet another surprise for you." Looking her full in the face, he gave her a smile he hoped was reassuring.

Lavonia eyed the clearing. "But we have no chaperone."

"Quite true. But I would not wish your sister to suffer another bout of illness as a result of an outdoor excursion."

"Agreed. Perhaps Helen—"

"Do you indeed want your cousin to join us?"

She hesitated. "Her presence would assure—"

"Nothing. Except perhaps some entertainment. We could find some amusement in watching her dramatics, *n'est pas?*"

"Soidisant." A roll of her eyes and a slight curl of her lips confirmed that she agreed.

"Now for the reason I brought you here." Reaching behind the seat, William pulled out a picnic basket and set it on his lap. "Will you consent to dine with me today, Miss Lavonia Penn?"

After the slightest pause, she answered, *"Oui, Monsieur."*

With a gallant wave of one hand, he extended the other to assist her from the carriage. The mere touch of her soft fingers sent a feeling that could only be described as a bolt of lightning through his being. So as not to lose his composure, he hastened to tie his faithful horse, General, to a sturdy pine tree. After stroking General a few times on his chestnut brown neck and speaking words of praise to the animal, William turned his attention to Lavonia, who had been observing him in silence, a smile on her face.

Choosing a level spot in the shade, William placed an old blue wool blanket on the ground and motioned for her to sit upon it. Before taking his own seat, he set a smaller embroidered white linen tablecloth next to her and two matching napkins on top.

"I did not imagine a bachelor would be so well equipped," she noted.

"I am afraid I must confess to not being as prepared as you imagine, Miss Penn. I borrowed these from my landlady."

Lavonia looked suspicious. "With her consent, of course."

"Let us just say, with the same 'by your leave' as your cousin gave you to be with me."

"Touché." She watched him take several slices of cold roast and a small round of fresh sourdough bread from the basket. A bunch of red grapes, enough to provide ample servings for them both, emerged. Upon eyeing them, a look of delight crossed her lovely features. "What luxury, to partake of such beautiful grapes this early in the season. Your landlady must run a lavish establishment."

Had he already been eating the grapes, William would have choked with laughter. "Mrs. Potter's boarding establishment is hardly a lavish place. In fact, I suspect my comrades there will be feasting on porridge tonight." Plucking one of the grapes, he held it up for inspection. "These grapes, *ma cherie,* were purchased from the market, at a very steep price. Imported from Italy, or so the merchant said."

Lavonia's mouth formed a small circle. "Then I shall eat them very slowly."

"Indulge as you like, as long as you enjoy them." Searching

near the bottom of the basket, he found a silver flask wrapped in a napkin. Though it was not as chilly as when he packed it, the bottle was still cool, much to his satisfaction.

"What is in there?" More than a little admonition colored Lavonia's voice.

"Le cidre, naturellement." To prove he was telling the truth, he withdrew a set of silver goblets and poured a few swallows of cider into each. He handed her a glass. "Were you expecting, say, a smooth cognac?" he asked, knowing well that their faith did not permit them to drink, nor to purchase or sell, intoxicating beverages.

She narrowed her eyes. "You!" Though she seemed to be attempting to sound serious, a peal of merriment escaped her lips.

He raised his glass in a toast. "To beauty."

"To beauty."

Though she made a show of looking at the blossoming trees, her cheeks nevertheless turned a most appealing shade of red. Then their eyes locked. He wished the moment could last an eternity.

Breaking free from his gaze, she turned her attention to the roast. "Let us not forget this delicious food. It would be most regrettable if your trouble were for naught."

William took a piece of bread and bit into it as he watched Lavonia place a thin slice of beef on her bread, then partake of it with delicate bites. He found himself imagining what it would be like to share every meal with her. With Lavonia as his dinner companion, their earlier topic of conversation almost faded from William's memory. He hoped she could forget, too.

"This is indeed the finest beef I have ever tasted," she said.

Realizing Lavonia wasn't given to hyperbole, William smiled with pleasure. Every penny he spent bribing Miss Potter's cook to bake the roast to perfection had been worth the price.

Having satiated her appetite, Lavonia stared at the sky. She was silent for a time before surveying the grandeur around them. "And you selected the perfect place to picnic."

"*Merci.*"

"And," she ventured, "this is a most ideal place to hear the reading of poetry. Perhaps one written by Dr. William Amory, presented in its entirety?"

"I am not much of a poet," he protested, even though her question pleased him. "Do you really wish to hear my ramblings?"

"Of course!"

"By happenstance, I have the poem with me today," he said, keeping his voice light to downplay that he had brought it in case she inquired. Whipping the paper out of a coat pocket, he proceeded to unfold it with flourish. He cleared his throat as if preparing for a great ceremony.

Lavonia giggled, but his look of mock admonishment caused her to put on a straight face.

He read:

I met an angel here today
  Comforting her sister's heart.
She knew not that she pierced mine own.
  Or how it cries when we must part—

In the foreground of my mind
  I hold a watercolor view
And long to sharpen its image
  As I have been dreaming of you.

"Such a beautiful poem," she whispered. "No one has ever written a verse to me."

"Then the men of your past acquaintance must have been both blind and dull."

"I must say, I can see why it is rumored you are quite the ladies' man." She threw him a crooked smile, finished the last drops of cider remaining in her goblet, and patted her lips dry.

Jarred by her observation, William didn't answer right away. Instead, he swirled his half goblet of cider in circles, causing the liquid to swish gently. Her revelation came as no surprise. Though many a woman had batted her eyes at him, even at the height of his roguish ways, William seldom accepted their unspoken invitations. Yet he knew his rakish reputation remained bloated beyond reality and persisted even though God had changed his life years ago.

Wondering what details Lavonia knew, he decided on a neutral response. "So that is what you heard?"

A nod was her only answer.

"The rumors must not have frightened you very gravely. You are here with me today."

"As you delight in reminding me, I cannot afford to be frightened if I plan to pursue a career on the mission field."

He waited, wondering whether she would admonish, judge, confront, or query him about his past. Or perhaps she would do all of those things. Mindlessly, he poured himself another glass of cider and held it, pretending to be absorbed in the bark of a nearby pine tree. Finally, when her silence lengthened and he was certain Lavonia had no plans to search him for answers, William breathed a sigh of relief. "Well," he finally said, "I am glad we got that unpleasantness out of the way." Lifting his goblet in her direction, he gave her a nod before finishing his liquid refreshment.

"So am I."

Relaxed for the first time since the topic of his past indiscretions had been raised, William focused on the loveliness of the one who shared his meal. He stared at her profile as she concentrated on a windblown tuft of grass. He couldn't help but think her portrait would make the perfect cameo brooch, raised in ivory, set on a background of blue. Her dark curls, flawless in their coiffure, her straight nose, and lips that protruded just enough to add interest, formed a beautiful silhouette.

Her lips moved, breaking the image he had in his mind's eye. She didn't look at him as she added, "But that is not all."

He felt his stomach do a somersault. "That is not all? Whatever do you mean?"

"I heard something else." She looked him full in the face. "Is it true you grew up in an orphanage?"

He averted his eyes. "It is true." He realized his voice was more abrupt than he meant it to be.

"That must have been a dreadful experience."

Encouraged by her sympathetic tone, he looked up at her. Rather than seeming shocked or judgmental, Lavonia's face was soft with compassion. He held his gaze upon her for a moment, not ready to answer.

"Tell me, what was it like?"

Too busy now living his life and pursuing his art and medical studies, William seldom dwelt on the past and had not thought about the orphanage in years. Lavonia's inquiry brought back a deluge of memories. He recalled Christmases fortified with gifts donated by the wealthy, some well-meaning, but most wanting to purchase freedom from the guilty knowledge that their own fortunes allowed themselves lives of luxury. Wealthy people who forgot about the orphans the rest of the year, as if the stomachs of parentless children growled with hunger only on Christmas day.

With few exceptions, the boys living in the home fended for themselves. Vegetable gardens were planted each season to assure a winter stock of food. Cows were milked. Chickens were fed. Nothing was wasted. Not food, and certainly not the cast-off clothing that was usually worn by several of the boys before one of the matrons finally declared it too ragged to be of further use.

He remembered the other orphans. Some were lucky enough to be adopted. Others, not so lucky, died before they reached adulthood. Still others, like William, were never rescued from the boy's home because they were too old, too frail, or not cherubic enough in manner or appearance to win the affections of prospective parents.

Finally, he spoke. "Do you wish to work with orphans, Miss Penn?"

She seemed surprised by his question. "Why, I had not given that prospect much thought."

"Then there is no need for me to dwell on the details. I am just grateful I did not end up as a street urchin. And I am thankful that my circumstances, though undesirable, did secure me a benefactor in later years."

"So no one ever showed any interest in adopting you." A quizzical expression indicated Lavonia had trouble believing her own observation.

"No." Encouraged by Lavonia's prodding, he continued, "They say I was a thin and sickly infant, and colicky, as well. My frailty and constant crying were apparently enough to keep even the most determined adoptive parents from taking a chance on me. By the time I outgrew my maladies and developed enough muscle to assure my continued health, I was too old to attract any attention."

"How awful."

William shrugged. "It seemed awful at the time, but it was my sicknesses that encouraged my interest in medicine. You see, I want to help others who are like I once was. And it was my desire to pursue medicine that brought me to my benefactor."

"Philemon Midas."

He nodded.

"Tell me, how did he find out about you?"

"Apparently, someone at the orphanage told him about my ambitions and he thought me worthy enough to secure his help. He became my benefactor when I was in my teen years, which assured my schooling was sufficient to prepare me for higher education. Later, his sterling support provided me with an education at Oxford."

"So he helped you all those years, and you never discovered anything about him, other than his name and the fact that he lived in Dover?" she asked.

"Regrettably, no."

"Were you never curious enough to try to meet him in person?"

"Certainly," he responded. "If for no other reason, I wanted to thank him. Of course, I wrote him many letters of gratitude, and I made certain to keep him apprised about my progress in my studies, but writing those letters could never replace seeing him, even if only to shake his hand."

"But the letters. Did he not send you any correspondence in return?"

"Once, upon my graduation from Oxford. I cherish that letter more than any other material possession I own." Then he remembered the ring that had been his mother's. "Almost." Ignoring Lavonia's puzzled expression, he continued, "After graduation, my interest in him intensified. Perhaps because of the letter."

"No doubt."

He stared into her blue eyes, so sympathetic he couldn't resist them. "Miss Penn, would you mind terribly if I shared a confidence with you?"

"Not at all."

"I know this will sound ludicrous, but remember, I was young." He took a breath. "During that time, I burned with the desire to meet this man. I even fantasized that Philemon

Midas could be my father." Afraid she would laugh at his silly illusion, he cast his gaze away from her face to the corner of the tablecloth.

"There is no shame in your dream. For why would you not wish to find your own father?" She placed a gentle hand on top of his. "Perhaps Philemon Midas is your father?"

"No. One of the matrons at the orphanage took pity on me when she learned of my fantasy. She showed me a letter from my father."

Lavonia gasped. "But I thought no one knew."

"No one did, for many years. But the letter arrived soon after I had left the orphanage. He wrote it on his deathbed, apparently in a fit of conscience for having lived a life of ease abroad while I was left to fend for myself."

"He should have felt guilty for not taking responsibility for you." Anger was evident on her face. "Why did he not?"

"His letter said he wanted to be a father. And he wanted to marry my mother."

"So they really were in love?"

"I believe they were. Certainly they were too young to consider money and position over their feelings for each other. But when my grandfather discovered she was merely a chamber maid, he sent my father abroad and dismissed her from his employ. They never saw each other again. She died shortly after my birth."

Tears misted Lavonia's eyes. "If only she could have seen what a fine gentleman you are now."

"A fine gentleman? The stock of an idle, irresponsible man of the world and an impoverished domestic servant?" William laughed, bitterness coloring every note. With his fingertips, he gently guided Lavonia's delicate chin in his direction, forcing her to look him full in the face. "The gentleman you see before you, Miss Penn, would not even gain admittance into the humblest home if not for his ability to heal. And he undoubtedly would be spurned from the homes of the wealthy, except for his ability to paint portraits." Taking his fingers from her face, he rose to his feet and stood before her. "Your cousin is right, Miss Penn. I am not worthy of you."

"I care not what anyone else thinks." Lavonia stood up, her eyes meeting his. Her voice was filled with so much conviction, he almost believed her.

"Perhaps you do not, but Helen does. And when all is said and done, that is all that matters." His heart ached at the thought that their rendezvous had been a mistake, that he had been a fool to think himself worthy of her. For Lavonia's sake, he knew he must offer her no further encouragement. He tilted his head in General's direction. "Get into the carriage. I shall take you home."

Certain his abrupt manner had convinced Lavonia to submit without protest, William turned his back toward her and tossed the remains of the picnic into the basket. He turned to leave, but to his astonishment, she had not moved. He kept his voice authoritative. "Get in the carriage, I tell you."

"I will not." She planted her feet on the ground for emphasis.

"While your fiery performances are not without a degree of charm, I am in no humor to witness a tantrum today. You will get in the carriage, even if I must carry you." He let the basket and blanket drop to the ground to prove he was serious.

Lavonia's response was to lift her chin an inch higher.

"All right, if you insist." William strode toward her and lifted her light form in his arms. She pounded her fists into his chest with amazing strength and squirmed to be released. By force of will, he ignored the blows and carried her toward the carriage.

"Let me go!"

"I told you I would carry you if I must." Complying with her demand, he set her feet on the grass beside the carriage.

"That should prove I am serious."

"So it shall." Sparks of rage flew from her eyes. "And this shall prove you are worthy of me!"

Before William knew what was happening, Lavonia wrapped her arms around his neck and kissed him firmly on the lips.

thirteen

William's lips were unexpectedly soft, but as he returned Lavonia's kiss, his strong body, so near to hers, left no doubt he was a man. "William," she breathed.

At the sound of his name, he responded by pulling her closer to him. "Lavonia."

Never had her name sounded so sweet! Every part of her wanted to melt in his embrace, but she knew she had to tear herself away from him. Against her will, she pressed a hand against his chest and pushed. Taken by surprise, he stepped back from her.

"What was that?" he asked.

"Exactly what I said. Proof that you are worthy of me." Though she was trying to keep her voice casual, she couldn't keep from straightening her bonnet, sweeping the sides of her dark chignon, pulling her lightweight shawl around her shoulders, and running her hands over her waist and hips to smooth the flowing skirt on her empire-style dress. Her heart was racing.

"A modest assessment of yourself, indeed." His violet eyes sparkled with mischief. "I hope this is not the way you prove your point to every man you meet."

His teasing had not been the reaction she had expected, or wanted. Feeling a surge of vexation, she shot him a withering look. "If that is what you think, then you can follow through with your original plan to take me home." She had one foot in midair before a better idea occurred to her. "Come to think of it, I shall walk home."

Though she nodded curtly in his direction to signal her

determination, her plan was thwarted when William picked her up and set her back into place in his carriage. "No lady who accompanies me to a worship service shall journey home alone. You shall stay there, Miss Penn."

His voice was firm enough to whip Lavonia into submission. Not that she had been eager to walk home in her Sunday dress shoes, on any account. Averting her eyes to focus on anything but him, she noticed the picnic basket still on the ground. "Certainly a fine gentleman such as yourself," she said, allowing sarcasm not previously present to color her voice, "should desire to return the items he secretly 'borrowed' from his landlady."

A contrite look crossed his face. Retrieving the basket in haste, he tossed it into the carriage. His eyes never left her as he untied General from the tree.

"You are so watchful," she noted. "Do you think I plan to escape?"

"Perhaps." Taking his place beside her, he noted, "You are a bit *imprèvisible, oui?*"

Lavonia felt her cheeks flush when he spoke the truth. She had indeed acted on impulse by kissing him.

Without warning, he placed his hand upon hers. "One of your finer qualities, I must say."

She jerked her hand from his grasp. "Stop mocking me!"

"I am not mocking you." He looked at her full in the face. "I am truly sorry I offended you just now, and with my jesting earlier. I confess, your—emotion—astonished me greatly. I am afraid I did not respond in the proper manner, as the gentleman you claim me to be would have."

He clicked his tongue as a signal for General to begin his trot home.

"And how would a gentleman have responded?"

"With shock, I suppose."

Lavonia remembered the astonished look on his face. "If

that is so, then you are indeed a gentleman."

"Is that your only evidence?"

Though taken aback by his inquiry, Lavonia could see by his serious expression that William sought an honest answer. She thought for a moment. "You were born of a nobleman."

"But, I am sorry to say, he was no gentleman."

"Well then, despite what you say about your checkered reputation, during the times we have been together, your behavior has always been quite exemplary. Indeed, I believe you have overcome your past."

"Do you?" He seemed surprised.

"Yes. If you had not, would you have taken me to a church meeting today?" Before he could answer her question, Lavonia continued, "I must confess, ever since we worshiped together, one question has burned in my mind. Might I ask how you came to accept the Lord as your Savior?"

"My story is long. Do you really wish to know?"

"Yes. And in any event, am I not a bit of a captive audience?" She flashed him a teasing smile.

"Captive or not, I shall spare you a verbal tome by giving you the condensed version. It began with the dear matrons who ran the orphanage. They had adopted the Methodist faith, and part of their mission was to teach it to us boys." He rolled his eyes. "Although I must say, at times that seemed their only mission."

Lavonia giggled.

"It pains me to admit this now. But even though I was a professing Christian, in reality I rebelled against their strict rules. By the time I left the orphanage, I had abandoned the idea of coming to a saving knowledge of Christ."

"So what made you change your mind?"

"One afternoon when I was visiting a patient, a bull broke out of his fence, chased me, knocked me to the ground, and stomped my leg."

The image made Lavonia cringe. "How dreadful!"

"Indeed. The attending physician was certain my leg would become infected with gangrene and would need to be amputated, and I agreed with his diagnosis. I was devastated. At the time, I would have preferred death over losing my leg. Perhaps that is why I refused to give up. I did what I had learned as a child to do in desperate times. I prayed to the Lord."

Lavonia glanced at William's legs. Even underneath his breeches, anyone could see they were in fine form. "Obviously, He answered your prayer."

"I admit, I was surprised. The Lord and I were not on the best of terms, thanks to my neglect of Him. But He was merciful. He gave me a second chance, and I knew it. I wanted to do something to thank Him."

"What did you do?" she prodded.

"I resolved to read the whole of Scripture."

His answer was a disappointment. "An admirable goal, but something certainly any Christian should do."

"Yes, but it was not so easy for me. I was a busy man, doing important work. Or so I thought. I was not willing to relinquish time I could be visiting patients or painting, so I gave up my Friday evening card games."

"Cards! William, how could you?"

"To the unsaved, such trivial pursuits seem merely a pleasant diversion, not a dire sin." He gave her an inquiring look. "Did you not give up any vice when you accepted the Lord?"

Lavonia remained silent.

"Certainly women of your station are not customarily given to strong drink or card playing, but perhaps there was a vexing habit the Lord helped you conquer?"

"I am afraid I have no colorful account to share. My testimony is that of a sheltered girl who grew up, always under the guidance of devout parents, within the Christian faith." She looked at her feet. "Although I have been asking the

Holy Spirit to help me with my impulsiveness."

"Give Him time." William chuckled.

Her spontaneous kiss too fresh in her mind, Lavonia was eager to divert the attention back to William. "Did you read the entire Word of God?"

"Yes, much to my surprise. I was certain I would be bored with it. The idea of studying ancient laws and learning all about rules I had little desire to obey held limited appeal for me. But when I began delving into the teachings of Jesus, I was drawn to their wisdom. There was no turning back. I read diligently, in every spare moment. Once I had read the Bible from cover to cover, I was committed to the Lord not just because He had saved my leg, but because through His Word, He had entered my heart."

"What a beautiful testimony, William. Thank you for sharing it with me." Her voice soft, this time it was she who placed her hand upon his. Though hers was now covered in the kidskin she wore on Sundays and his was gloved in leather suitable for driving, the warmth of his hand penetrated hers.

"So you forgive me, then?"

She gave his hand a squeeze before letting it go. "Of course." A prick of conscience caused her to bite her lip. "For you are a gentleman by not mentioning how I momentarily forgot how to act like a lady."

"Think nothing more of it." Though his words were reassuring, she didn't like the knowing smile that touched his lips.

"Before we close the subject, Dr. Amory, I want you to know I do not conduct myself in such a manner often. In fact, before today, I have never behaved that way at all. Ever." Realizing her face was sure to be the color of rubies, she made a show of observing a herd of grazing sheep as the carriage passed.

"Never?" she heard him ask.

"Never." Eyeing him with her peripheral vision, she saw William's eyebrows shoot up as if he were surprised.

"That was your first kiss?"

"Yes," she muttered, certain that her face had flushed from the color of rubies to the hue of fully ripe beets.

"Pity. Had I known, I would have executed the deed with far more care." The mischief in his violet eyes was evident as he cut his glance to her. "Shall I stop the carriage so we might try again?"

She narrowed her eyes and folded her arms tightly across her chest. "No, you may not!"

"A pity indeed." A chuckle brought a merry light to his eyes and countenance.

Still blushing but no longer on the defensive, she let her hands rest in her lap and she remained silent, enjoying the rest of the short journey. She knew her peace wouldn't last long. Helen's certain wrath awaited.

&

As soon as she walked in the door, Lavonia was ambushed by the maid, who had been instructed to tell Lavonia to go to the drawing room forthwith. Dreading the encounter but at the same time wanting to get it over, Lavonia made haste. When she reached the French doors, she took in a breath, steadying her mind for what was to come.

Peering through the glass, she witnessed the picture of domestic tranquillity. Comfortable in his overstuffed chair, Luke was reading a London newspaper as he puffed on a walnut pipe. Seated in the matching chair beside her husband was Helen, immersed in one of her novels. Across the room on the davenport sat Katherine, lost in the art of crocheting delicate doilies. The scene seemed so peaceful, so typical of a Sunday afternoon at the Syms estate, that Lavonia decided to keep her greeting light.

"Comment allez-vous?"

As soon as Helen heard Lavonia's voice, she jumped from her seat. Pausing just long enough to set her book on a nearby table, she didn't bother to mark the page she was reading. "So finally you see fit to return to us, Lavonia." Her eyes narrowed. "What is the meaning of this? What made you go out alone without so much as a 'by your leave'?"

"I was so worried, Vonnie. I thought you might have been killed!" Having issued her complaint, Katherine began sobbing into her kerchief, punctuating each utterance with a shake of her thin shoulders.

Lavonia marveled at the sudden change in the room. "Were you really so frantic? Why, when I looked in just a moment ago, you seemed quite peaceful, as if you had not a care in the world."

"We had to do something to occupy our time," Helen said. "Since you failed to inform us of your plans, we had no idea when you might return."

"Or if you would return," Katherine added. "Where were you?"

"I was at church." Lavonia tilted her head upward ever so slightly.

"Church? But all of us went to worship hours ago."

"It was an afternoon service. At the Stone place."

Helen's eyes flashed with anger. "Who told you about the Stone place?" she huffed.

"So you knew about the services there." Lavonia didn't bother to ask her cousin why she hadn't told her about them. She was well aware that Helen wished her to return to the Anglican faith.

"Who told you?"

Lavonia took a breath. "Dr. Amory."

"That snake." Helen's chest began to heave. "I might have known."

Luke patted her shoulder. "There, there, *ma cherie*. There is no need to upset yourself."

"No, there is not," Lavonia said. "Although I am sorry I worried you. I beg your forgiveness. Now, if you will excuse me, I would like to rest." Lavonia placed her hand on the doorknob to exit.

"There, you see?" Luke asked Helen. "All she did was attend a church service. There was nothing to worry about, all along."

"Is that so?" Helen's head snapped in Lavonia's direction. "Did the doctor escort you?"

She nodded, her heart sinking with the realization that all was not yet well.

"Then where is he?" Luke asked.

"He has gone home."

"Home? I should say, he acted in a most untoward fashion, to allow you to walk to your door unescorted," he noted.

"He is not to blame. He asked to accompany me to the door, but I was the one who insisted he not stay." Though Lavonia spoke the truth, she wished William were standing beside her at that moment. She hadn't anticipated the fervor of the inquisition she now faced.

Luke's eyes widened. "Are you saying he offended you so much you did not wish him to enter our home?"

"No, not at all—"

"He did not sully your virtue, did he?" Helen's voice was high-pitched. Snapping open her fan, she began waving it frantically in front of her face as if she were facing a burst of flame.

"Indeed not."

Helen looked over at Katherine, then returned her attention to Lavonia. "I realize you must speak with the utmost delicacy in front of your sweet maiden sister."

Lavonia rolled her eyes at Helen's description. "I have

nothing to say that is too vulgar for Katherine's ears."

Helen's eyebrows arched. "I understand, Lavonia." She turned to Katherine. "*Ma cherie,* allow us to speak alone, *s'il vous plait.*"

Having acquired Helen's dramatic habit, Katherine opened her own fan and swished it back and forth in front of her face. "Surely my sister's adventure was not so wicked that I must be shielded from the details!"

"Let me be the judge of that," Helen snapped. She nodded in her younger cousin's direction. "Please, Katherine."

Pouting, Katherine exited as she was asked. As soon as the door of the drawing room shut behind her, Helen hissed, "She holds you in such high esteem. Why do you betray her?"

"But I did not betray her!"

"Conducting a private rendezvous with a known rake of undetermined pedigree is hardly exemplary behavior," Luke observed.

"A known rake? Who is it that knows William Amory?"

"Many know him. For one, your Uncle Joseph."

Lavonia rolled her eyes. She would never rely upon his judgment. "And what does Uncle Joseph know?"

"I know not the details," Luke admitted through tightened lips, "but I had the distinct feeling he was not pleased to see the doctor when he last visited."

"*Oui,*" agreed Helen.

"That is nebulous speculation indeed," Lavonia argued.

"But Vicar Gladstone knows the doctor well, I assume, to recommend that I commission his cousin to paint my own wife's portrait rather than the doctor."

"And the vicar had no motive for wanting the commission to be paid his cousin rather than a doctor who does not even attend his church?" Lavonia challenged him. When he didn't respond, she added, "Certainly, you do not know him, if you rely solely on gossips who have nothing better to do than to spread lies for their personal gain!"

"Of course he knows the doctor," Helen defended her husband. "We all are acquainted with him. Why, he has even dined with us."

"Upon your invitation, Lavonia. Not mine," Luke reminded her.

Refusing to be put off by his pointed comment, Lavonia squared her shoulders. "If he is so shameful, then why do you even invite his acquaintance?"

"Why, because he is the finest doctor in the region. And his talent for portraiture speaks for itself."

Luke's words brought back William's earlier words. *The gentleman you see before you, Miss Penn, would not even gain admittance into the humblest home if not for his ability to heal. And he undoubtedly would be spurned from the homes of the wealthy, except for his ability to paint portraits.*

So William's observations were no exaggeration. She felt her chest tighten.

Helen's voice interrupted her musings, "It is true that William Amory is a fine doctor. I have told you so myself, many times. No one would dispute that." Stepping toward Lavonia, Helen placed what was meant to be a consoling hand on her shoulder. Her tone became sympathetic. "I am certain you are grateful to him for helping your sister. But gratitude need only go so far. There is no need to mingle with the lower classes just because they have done you a favor, *ma cherie.*"

Only sheer force of will restrained Lavonia from blurting William's secret, that his father had been of more noble station than Helen could ever hope to be. As much as Lavonia wished Helen could be her ally, if her opinion changed merely because of William's lineage and not because of his heart, the victory would be hollow indeed.

"Listen to your cousin. She knows how to make a fine match." Luke's voice was conciliatory, and he smiled as if her transgression were forgiven. "Helen, darling," Luke continued, "Why do you not plan a gala in honor of our house guests? Just a few friends who might prove prospective and appropriate suitors."

The delight on Helen's face was obvious. "What a pleasing notion!"

"No, it is not," Lavonia snapped.

Helen looked at her, askance. "Whatever do you mean?"

Lavonia softened her tone. "Though I am grateful to you for your kind intentions, I have no desire for a party of any sort."

"Do you fear it may not seem correct to be the guest of honor at a party so soon after you have come out of deep mourning? I do understand," Helen consoled her. "But I assure you, we shall keep the event within the confines of what is proper."

Lavonia wondered when Helen would ever see that the world's idea of what is proper had little effect upon her. "That is not the reason."

"Then what?"

Luke intervened. "If you think I will permit you to traipse around with that rapscallion, then you are mistaken."

"What have you to say about my suitors?" Lavonia challenged.

"Since I am your closest male relative, everything."

"I beg to differ. Uncle Joseph is my closest male relative."

Luke chuckled. "And you believe your uncle will give his consent to any association with this doctor?"

Recalling the obvious animosity she had witnessed between William and her uncle, Lavonia knew Luke was right. He would never concede.

Luke threw her a triumphant smile. "I shall interpret your silence as agreement."

"Well, now," Helen said, closing her fan. "What a relief to

have that matter settled. You do know, dear, we have your best interests—and the best interests of our family's good name and reputation—at heart. It would be tragic indeed to have you be seen socializing with such a man. I only pray no one of any importance saw you today."

As Lavonia thought about the devout crowd of worshipers at the church service, her rage at her cousin's snobbishness increased. "No one you would think is of any importance."

Helen smiled. "Very well, then. All is forgiven."

"As long as you never see the doctor again," Luke added.

"I will consent to no such thing!"

"But why not, Lavonia?" Helen asked.

Lavonia didn't hesitate to answer. "Because, my dear cousin, I love him."

fourteen

Lavonia couldn't believe what she had just said. But once spoken, it was too late to take back her words.

Helen didn't hesitate to fly into an apoplectic fit. "Love him? Certainly not! I will not allow it!" She stood and stamped her foot for emphasis.

"But, but—I do!" For the first time, Lavonia realized that she did indeed mean what she said. She loved William Amory. And though Helen and Luke should not have been the first to hear her declaration, expressing her emotion left her feeling more free than she had felt in a long time.

Helen's breathing became ragged. "This should have never happened. He should never have kidnapped you like that. We should have been keeping a closer eye on him. This is all our fault!"

"No, Helen, there is no one to blame," Lavonia insisted.

"What would your dear parents say if they knew how we had let you run wild?" Helen agonized. "What will people say about such an ill-suited match?"

Placing a hand on each of Helen's shoulders, Luke guided her to the davenport. "Helen, do try to calm yourself," he said softly.

Nodding, she withdrew the bottle of smelling salts she always carried and inhaled. As she regained her composure, Luke tried to remain the voice of reason. "Lavonia, let us sit down and discuss this matter in a rational manner, as befitting adults." Motioning for her to sit in the chair next to his, he waited for her to acquiesce before he took his seat.

Though Lavonia had no wish to discuss anything about

William with them, she could see Luke was making every effort to keep his household from erupting into a complete uproar. She sat, deciding to at least give him a hearing.

"Do you realize that you have not known Dr. Amory very long?" he began.

"There is no set time to determine one's true love, except the time God allots." She searched her memory for examples. "Remember Isaac? His wife Rebekah was chosen for him by a servant of Abraham. Her father agreed to let Rebekah leave his home to marry Isaac, sight unseen. And later, her son, Jacob had only known Rachel a month before he asked Laban to give him her hand as wages for his labor."

"Romantic Bible tales indeed, but both of those marriages took place in a culture and time much different from ours," Luke pointed out.

"I have no dispute with you on that point," Lavonia agreed. "But though times change, God remains the same. Certainly you recall that Jesus is recorded in three of the Gospel books, Matthew, Mark, and Luke, as saying, 'Heaven and earth shall pass away, but my words shall not pass away.' "

"Perhaps. But in the case of both betrothals you cite, the prospective bridegroom stated his intent, either directly or through a representative. However, in your case, Dr. Amory has not seen me to express any such intention toward you. So how can you be certain your feelings are reciprocated?"

Lavonia felt heat rising to her cheeks. "I suppose I have no way of knowing."

"I see." He paused, presumably to allow her time to absorb the impact of his observation. "In that light, do you think it wise to pin all of your hopes on this man?"

The clear logic of his argument made her squirm. Unable to give him a satisfactory answer, she stared at the botanical pattern on the gold-and-black Persian rug.

"Lavonia, you are not experienced in the ways of the world.

And from what I have seen since you have been here with us, you have a pure heart. One that can be easily broken, I fear. You do realize it is not my wish for you to be taken advantage of in any way, particularly while you are a guest in my house."

Her eyes still fixated on the rug, Lavonia nodded.

"But you need not fear. What you told us here today shall remain in our confidence. We shall never tell a soul, not even your sister. It is not our wish for you to be embarrassed." Reaching over, Luke gave her a couple of reassuring pats on the hand.

"Thank you," she muttered, realizing that was the expected response.

"However, whatever your feelings are for the doctor, I recommend that you not see him again."

She raised her eyes to his. "But—"

His voice was sharp. "Not because of the doctor's character or station. But because I believe you need time away from him to take assessment of your feelings. See if they are real. See if they are indeed from God." His countenance took on a pleading look. "Will you do that? Not for us, but for yourself?"

Lavonia thought for a moment. Perhaps Luke was right. Her feelings had come upon her quickly, and she hadn't taken the time to think about them, or to ask the Lord about them. Finally she nodded. "All right. I will not try to see him for a while."

As soon as she made her promise, she wondered how she could possibly keep her word.

≈

As soon as Lavonia agreed not to see William, Luke had dispatched a letter to him with express instructions to show restraint toward Miss Lavonia Penn. With all hopes shattered that she would see William by accident, Lavonia did everything in her power to keep her mind from thoughts of him, but nothing she did—or didn't do—seemed to help. Thankfully, Helen didn't seem to notice her moods. Even better, she made no further comments about William. Lavonia wondered if perhaps Luke had advised her not to put Lavonia in the position of defending him. Whatever the reason for Helen's discretion, Lavonia was grateful.

The following Sunday she wished to slip out of the house long enough to go to the worship service at the Stones'. Yet each time there was an opportunity, Helen, Luke, or Katherine would intervene. Though they didn't say it, Lavonia knew they were keeping a close watch on her, lest she stray from her promise. She wondered if he went to the service without her. Though her heart ached to be with him, she prayed that he went. At least one of them should have the edification of God's community of believers.

By late afternoon, when she had given up all plans for escape, Lavonia sat with the others in the drawing room. With the ladies' permission, Luke lit the tobacco and puffed, sending smoke throughout the small room. Helen was reading, while Katherine searched her sewing basket and extracted a skein of white yarn. Since each was immersed in singular pursuits, Lavonia knew she could read her Bible in comfortable silence.

Closing her eyes, she silently asked God to speak to her as she committed her devotional time to Him. Then, opening her eyes, she slipped her thumb at a random place in the Holy Book. It fell open to Song of Solomon 5:2: "I sleep, but my heart waketh: it is the voice of my beloved that knocketh, saying, Open to me, my sister, my love, my dove, my undefiled: for my head is filled with dew, and my locks with the drops of the night."

Lavonia's eyes roved over the words until her mind was no longer upon them. Her father had said that though Song of Solomon seemed to be a romantic book on the surface, he believed it was an expression of love for the country of Israel rather than for a person. Yet as she read, Lavonia could think only of William.

She decided to try another passage. This time, she deliberately placed her thumb two thirds of the way through her Bible, knowing the page would fall in a Gospel or an epistle. As it opened, her eyes fell to Matthew 19:4: "And he answered and said unto them, Have ye not read, that he which made them at the beginning made them male and female, And said, For this cause shall a man leave father and mother, and shall cleave to his wife: and they twain shall be one flesh? Wherefore they are no more twain, but one flesh. What therefore God hath joined together, let not man put asunder."

Stifling an agitated breath, Lavonia couldn't help but wonder if God was trying to tell her not to give up, that William indeed was the one He had chosen for her.

A cough from Katherine caused her to abandon her musings. "My," she said, fanning smoke away from her face, "I do not mean to be ungracious, Luke, but the aroma from your pipe is not quite so pleasant today."

"I must agree," Helen said. "What do you think, Lavonia?"

"I have been too absorbed in my reading to notice until now." She took a deep breath, which resulted in a sudden coughing fit.

"Does that not answer your question?" Helen asked.

"*Je s'excuser,*" Luke apologized. "This is not my usual tobacco. A friend brought a jar of this blend from abroad. The blend is Turkish, and reputed to be of fine quality."

"It does not smell as if it is of fine quality," Helen noted, fanning smoke away from her face.

"Perhaps it did not travel well."

"*Oui!*" Katherine agreed before launching into a fresh fit of coughing. Rising from her seat, she begged their pardon and exited.

Noting that her sister's face had turned sanguine, Lavonia was worried. "Let me see how she is."

She found Katherine in the kitchen. Betsy was shooing her

out, although she had provided the girl with a glass of water.

"Feeling better, now?" Lavonia asked.

Taking a sip of water, Katherine shook her head. "Not very. My throat is clogged, and now I feel as though a headache is well on its way."

Lavonia was about to answer when she saw the cat rubbing against Katherine's dress. "Scat!"

"Must you frighten the poor cat?" Placing her glass of water on the dining room table, Katherine knelt down and, in an uncharacteristic show of affection, rubbed Snowball's white fur. Within moments, Katherine began to sneeze. Rising, she patted her nose with her kerchief.

Lavonia remembered the advice William had given her sister. "Did the doctor not tell you to stay away from the cat?"

Katherine pouted. "He suggested perhaps I should not live in a house with a cat. But I hardly see how I can tell my hostess to free herself of her own pet. In any event, he has no proof that the cat causes my headaches."

"You have a headache now, do you not?"

"I already had a headache. And you are not making it any better." Katherine shook her head in obvious agitation. "Honestly, Vonnie, I think you believe anything that man says!" Without waiting for Lavonia to retort, she swiveled toward the hallway. "If anyone cares, I shall be in my bedchamber, indisposed for the remainder of the afternoon."

❧

William was washing his brushes after a full day of painting at the Roths' when he received word to appear at the Syms estate. His heart singing, he hurried to complete his task.

"Perhaps she wants to see me after all," he muttered under his breath.

"What was that, Doctor?" Mrs. Roth queried.

He gave his head a quick shake, the physical motion transporting his mind back to reality. "Nothing, Mrs. Roth. I was just thinking aloud."

The matron's plain face was fixed in a worried expression, though William suspected her anxiety was tempered with a healthy dose of curiosity. "Is everything quite all right?"

"I am certain everything is quite all right, Mrs. Roth." Upon tossing his brushes in a wooden case, he tipped his hat and bade her good day.

Hopping astride General, he pulled the reins and gave the animal a sharp rap on the rump so he would move with haste. This was the message for which he had been waiting! To be summoned to the Syms' home.

William wondered if Lavonia had known how his heart had been broken when he received Luke's letter not to return to the estate. What had changed Luke's mind? The answer was only a few gallops away.

As he approached the walk leading to the verandah, he curtailed his eagerness lest he run like a schoolboy. After barely acknowledging the servant who answered the door, he awaited Lavonia's arrival in the parlor. His heart felt as though it would beat through his coat as the door creaked open.

"La—" he stopped himself short.

"You were expecting someone else?" Helen's stonefaced expression offered nothing in the way of either humor or sympathy.

Regaining his composure, he tipped his hat. "Good afternoon, Mrs. Syms."

"Afternoon." She greeted him with a curt nod.

He tried to keep his voice brisk. "I received a message to come here at once."

"Yes. Katherine is ill."

William's entire being felt heavy with disappointment, as though he could fall through the cracks in the floor. For an instant, he wished he could. "I am so sorry. Is she in her bed?"

"Yes. I shall accompany you there." She glanced at his

empty hands. "Have you no medical bag?"

A wave of chagrin swept over him. "I, I do not suppose so." His eyes met her steely gaze. "I was painting at the Roths, and did not stop to retrieve my bag. But I can still help Miss Penn," he hastened to add.

After shooting him a look filled with doubt, Helen led him up the stairs. William surveyed the house, hoping Lavonia would somehow appear out of nowhere to greet him. When she didn't, he set his mind on healing his patient.

They found Katherine asleep.

"Poor soul," Helen observed. "She has had so little rest all day."

Since she was sleeping on her back, William could see that Katherine's eyelids were swollen and her cheeks puffed so that her features seemed almost contorted. Every few breaths, she would snort in her sleep as if trying to clear her nose. "Has she been doing that all day?"

Helen nodded. "Since yesterday. That is when she first became ill."

"Do you know what caused it?"

"I do," a sweet voice interrupted.

He turned to see Lavonia standing in the doorway, a vision in flowing lavender. Her eyes sparkled like sapphires. Her skin was creamy and framed in dark ringlets. The mere sight of her caused his heart to pick up its pace once again. By sheer force of will, he kept his voice even. "Good afternoon, Miss Penn."

"Good afternoon, Dr. Amory."

Helen was not so congenial. "Lavonia, I thought I told you I would summon you if I needed you here."

"Yes, but I have been responsible for my sister's care for quite some time. I think it is best that I confer with the doctor." Her gaze diverted to William. "My sister had been exposed to smoke from stale tobacco in a closed room yesterday afternoon when she first complained of her headache. Then, against my counsel, she petted the cat, which brought on a sneezing fit. At that point, she retired to her bed and has been there ever since."

William turned to Helen. "I have given instructions for my patient to stay away from the cat. And though I know your husband enjoys his tobacco, his smoking seems to be contributing to her plight."

Helen gave him a sheepish shrug. *"Quel dommage!"*

"Your pity helps her not. I must ask that your husband smoke his cigars in private and that you keep the cat out of my patient's path. Or," he added, inclining his head to Lavonia, "you should find another relative with whom to stay."

"That would be your desire, *oui?*" Helen's eyes narrowed as she directed the question to the doctor.

"My desire is for my patient to recover. And she cannot in a house where my instructions are ignored." He nodded with an abrupt motion. "That is all." Pivoting toward Lavonia and the door, he strode toward her, intending to pass. With one sideways step, she blocked his path.

"Doctor."

"Yes?" His eyes met hers. For an instant, he thought he saw a spark of interest. Or was it his imagination? He knew he was not imagining her warmth, her sweet scent. Or the feelings of love now stirring within him.

"Is there anything at all I can do to help?"

He felt the corner of an envelope tap his waist. Realizing she was passing him a letter, he clutched the paper with a furtive motion. "Just do as I say." His brusque tone masked his emotion.

He had just hidden the letter in his vest pocket when Helen joined them, her prying eyes searching them closely. "Thank you, Doctor. That will be all."

William muttered a few pleasantries before making a hasty exit. He had to get home and read Lavonia's letter.

fifteen

After he secured General in his stall in Mrs. Potter's modest stable, William rushed to his room. Once the door closed behind him, he reached into his vest pocket and retrieved the letter. Not bothering to sit, he broke the wax seal bearing the Penn coat of arms and lifted the flap of the cream-colored paper. The scent of Lavonia's rosewater perfume clung to it, reminding him of how he longed to be close to her. Unfolding the enclosed note, he devoured the words, written in a careful feminine hand:

> William:
>   I am writing this because on Sunday past, I failed to make mention of news that could be of great import to you. I do not think it politic to share the details here, but suffice it to say, I have reason to believe your benefactor, Philemon Midas, is still alive. I pray this development will somehow be a blessing to you.
>
>   Yours,
>   Lavonia Penn

Reading the words over several times, William searched for any clue as to Lavonia's feelings. A wave of disappointment engulfed him when he realized the message contained not the slightest hint of her regard for him.

Remembering Lavonia's kiss, one that seemed so full of emotion, he wondered how she could have written him a letter so bloodless. She didn't seem to be a woman of easy virtue, or one who would make such a gesture to satisfy idle

151

curiosity. Could he have misjudged her? No, he didn't think so. Still, William was baffled.

"Why was she so secretive about passing the letter to me?" he wondered. "Could her furtiveness have some relation to the mysterious details she declined to reveal?"

At that moment, William resolved to see Lavonia again, regardless of the consequences. But first, he had an urgent errand to complete.

❧

The following week, Katherine burst onto the back patio, where Lavonia had taken a basket of mending so she could enjoy the warmth of the sun.

"Oh, Vonnie! The most wonderful thing has happened!" Clasping her hands to her chin, Katherine looked skyward. Obviously unable to contain her glee, she swayed back and forth.

Lavonia hadn't seen her sister so enthralled since she had been presented with a velvet-clad porcelain doll on her eighth birthday. Eager to discover the source of her sister's pleasure, Lavonia set the dress she was hemming in her lap. "What is it?"

"Osmond has asked Luke for permission to court me!" Exhaling dreamily, Katherine cast Lavonia a starry-eyed gaze. "Is that not wonderful?"

Remembering his unappealing looks, botched attempts at French, and longwinded prayers, Lavonia wondered how her sister could be so enamored with Vicar Gladstone. But the light in her eyes said she was.

Hesitating before weighing in with her opinion, Lavonia swallowed. "I must admit, Kitty, I had never envisioned you as a vicar's wife. And though his interest in you has not escaped my notice, I had no idea you desired his romantic attentions."

"Really?"

Lavonia nodded.

Exhaling, Katherine placed one hand on her chest. "What a relief to find I was not as transparent with my affections as I had feared."

Reflecting for a moment, Lavonia remembered the times Katherine had been dressed far too fancifully when she thought the vicar might visit. Her face would brighten at his appearance and, when addressing him, her voice would take on a melodious quality not present when she was complaining about her ills.

Lavonia was ashamed. Katherine's proclamation had forced her to realize she had been too involved in her personal turmoil to see that her sister was falling in love. Before articulating her opinion, Lavonia sent up a quick silent prayer for guidance.

"So, you indeed hold him in high regard?" Lavonia asked.

"Oh, yes! Unequivocally!"

"But you are accustomed to a degree of luxury. Trips abroad. Fine clothing. Superb food. Are you quite certain you will be content to live in a modest parsonage?"

"Oh, but did you not know? Osmond has his sights set on London. That is why he has been traveling so much in recent weeks."

"Yes, he did mention his aspirations." Lavonia bit her tongue to keep from commenting on his unbridled ambition.

"And of course, as a learned man of the clergy, he commands respect wherever he goes."

"Of course." She paused, sending up another prayer for guidance on what to say next. "Kitty, since we are sisters, I hope I may be frank."

"Certainly." Katherine stiffened.

"What if he fails to secure a London parish? Will you be happy living with him, regardless of his circumstances? And," she added, "what if circumstances became such that he needed to pursue a vocation apart from the Church?

Would you be as pleased to be his wife if he were to become a common laborer?"

When Katherine's eyes widened, Lavonia knew she had offered her sister a new perspective. "Of, of course." Then her face brightened. "But I cannot understand why Osmond would leave the Church. He loves his vocation—and the Lord—so!"

"Our Savior no doubt knows his heart. And certainly you are more well acquainted with the vicar than I."

"And I shall become even more well acquainted with him in the coming months, *oui?*" Katherine smiled.

"I only caution that if you develop any doubts or fears during your courtship, be certain they are allayed before agreeing to a betrothal."

"I will." She hurried to the wicker chair where Lavonia sat and knelt beside her. Katherine's eyes were wide with pleading. "Oh, say you are happy for me, Vonnie."

Lavonia failed to see what attraction such a man could hold for her sister. Yet she didn't have the heart to inflict upon her the same sorrow Luke and Helen were forcing her to endure with their opposition to William.

Lavonia gave Katherine the warmest smile she could muster. "Then, I am happy for you."

Katherine beamed. "Oh, thank you, Vonnie!" Leaning toward her, she gave Lavonia an embrace.

❧

"How was yer trip, doctor?" Mrs. Potter greeted him upon his return from Dover.

"Difficult," William revealed without thinking.

Her raised eyebrows invited further comment, but William was in no mood to share his disappointment, at least not with her.

He tipped his hat. "I thank you for your inquiry, Mrs. Potter, but I am afraid I should not prove much of a conversationalist tonight. By your leave, I shall not be joining the others at the dinner table."

"You'll be missin' chicken pie."

Though her chicken pie was among the more palatable in her repertoire, even that promise wasn't enough to lure him. "Sounds delicious. I regret I shall miss what promises to be a lovely meal. Please convey my excuses to the others. If I am summoned for a medical emergency, I can be found in my room. Otherwise, I do not wish to be disturbed."

Without further ado, he ascended the stairs, each board creaking in protest. The trip to Dover had been wearying physically, his failure to find the whereabouts of Philemon Midas only compounding his fatigue. Even thoughts of Lavonia didn't provide him with the usual burst of energy that could only have been explained by love.

If only I could see her. I know she has the answers. But I cannot. Her cousin has forbidden me, and her lack of passion for me was evident in her letter. Ever since receiving it, he couldn't reconcile his shock at the unfeeling letter with her warmth that previous Sunday afternoon. Yet, she had been as businesslike as his most disagreeable patient. He wondered how he could have misinterpreted her feelings.

Perhaps she is too embarrassed by her outburst of emotion to wish to see me again. Perhaps she thinks me a brute and wants to forget all about me. All indications point in that direction. He sighed. *If only I had not insisted we go on the picnic!*

Entering his stark room, he focused on the single bed. For once, the hard mattress looked appealing. "Perhaps after a good night's sleep," he muttered, "I shall possess the fortitude to renew my search."

But his leads were as exhausted as he. How could he ever find Philemon Midas without Lavonia's help? He was still mulling over the puzzle as he drifted into a dreamless sleep.

ta

Sitting on the wooden verandah swing, Lavonia was enjoying

one last peaceful time observing the Syms' front garden as her sister slept and her hosts enjoyed their usual early morning horseback ride. Rocking back and forth, Lavonia read the letter she had written to Jane to inform her that she couldn't afford the passage to America and would be remaining in England. She had been procrastinating on writing the letter. As a result, its arrival would be later than she had anticipated. But Jane knew Lavonia's plans weren't set, so she prayed any distress on her part would be minimal.

After almost two years of uncertainty, Lavonia was grateful that new plans had developed for her over the past week. Following her initial objections, Aunt Amelia's conscience had apparently been pricked so that she sent a letter asking Lavonia to live with her for an indefinite period of time. She had been particularly vexed that Katherine refused to come and do her bidding, and now claimed that Lavonia was "her favorite niece." Though her aunt had been careful to avoid mention of her expectations in the correspondence, Lavonia knew she would probably be doing most of the household tasks, at least until she found a post as a nanny or governess elsewhere. She didn't mind. The time had come for her to leave her cousin's home and pursue a life of her own.

Though minding and teaching the children of the upper classes was not the life, or the mission, Lavonia had promised her mother she would undertake, she was at peace. During her nightly prayers the previous week, she had given the decision over to the Lord. To follow her mother's ambition for her if the Lord didn't make such a provision would be nothing short of worshiping her over God. Lavonia was grateful that the Lord in His mercy had only taken her far from her mission in geography, not purpose. She looked forward to the opportunity to share His love with whatever children He saw fit to place in her charge.

The sound of hooves pounding on the drive barely disturbed

her, since she was expecting Luke and Helen to return from
their morning ride in due time. She looked up for an instant,
intent to bid them a good morning. Instead, what she saw
made her snap her head, her mouth dropping open with surprise. Her stomach felt as though it would flip through her
dress, right along with her beating heart.

"William!" She stood to greet him.

"So, you remember?" His teasing smile made her ache anew,
knowing this would be their last time together. With lithe steps,
he bounded onto the porch and took a place in an outdoor chair
adjacent to the swing. As quickly as it had appeared, his levity
evaporated. "Are your cousins home?"

"No. Do you wish to see them?"

"No. It is you I came to see." He took off his hat and held it
in his hands, a motion of humility she had never seen him
perform. "I know I have no right to come here like this, when
you have made it plain you do not wish to see me. But since
you were so kind as to tell me your suspicions about Philemon
Midas, I hope you will overlook my transgression. I assure
you, my intent is merely to inquire further about him. Nothing
more."

"Oh." Her heart sank. "Well, certainly I will do what I can
to help."

"And for that, I thank you. But first, I must apologize. Since
Mr. Syms informed me I was not to see you again, I realize I
must have somehow offended you during our past time together. I beg your pardon, Miss Penn. I would never intentionally do such a thing. I pray that enough time has passed now
that you will forgive me."

Lavonia was puzzled. Had her letter not conveyed to him
her interest in him and his affairs? "Why do you insist I do
not wish to see you? How can you believe that?"

"Your last correspondence to me indicated nothing otherwise."

"Do you not realize I feared someone else would see the

letter? I did not wish to vex my cousin. As you can imagine, the whole household was quite perturbed after they discovered I had stolen away to be with you."

"Oh." The relief on his face was evident. "In that case, I hope the scene was not too unpleasant."

At that moment, Helen and Luke turned the corner of the drive. "Hopefully no more unpleasant than the scene we are about to encounter," Lavonia observed.

As soon as they reached the front yard, Luke shouted, "What are you doing here, Amory?" He jumped off his horse and strode toward William.

He opened his mouth to defend himself, but Lavonia stopped him with a furtive tap on the small of his back. "Dr. Amory is here on a matter of business."

Luke's head snapped in Lavonia's direction. "What business could he possibly have with you?"

"*Vraiment.*" Helen appeared at his side. "That is what I would like to know."

"It is about the deed to my house. We want to see it."

"The deed?" Luke asked.

"I know it is in your possession. Uncle Joseph told me he left a spare set of papers with you." Though she spoke the truth, Lavonia prayed the Lord would forgive her for omitting the fact that she had also happened upon the papers in Luke's study.

"Why would you need to see the papers?" he asked. "Surely a woman need not bother herself with such matters."

"The deed is hers, in principle if not by law. I request that you show it to us immediately," William interjected.

"*Au contraire,* my good doctor. As the male head of this household, I am entrusted to keep the deed on behalf of both sisters. To obey your wish would be a violation of the trust of Miss Katherine, even if Miss Lavonia wishes you to see it."

"See what?" Appearing at the front door, Katherine was

bleary-eyed, her hair uncombed, and her dress disheveled, the obvious results of a hasty toilette.

Helen rushed to her side. "Katherine, why are you out of bed?"

"I heard voices. Is there some sort of dispute?"

"Mais non," Helen answered.

"Mais oui!" Lavonia contradicted her. "Katherine, I am glad you awoke. I have asked Luke to show us the deed of sale to the house. Do you have any objections?"

Despite a warning look from Luke, Katherine answered, "Of course not. But I see no reason why everyone must read it. Is something the matter?"

"There could be. I saw the deed," Lavonia told her. "It was signed by Philemon Midas."

Katherine paused, then a flash of memory flickered over her features. "Dr. Amory's benefactor? But I thought he was dead."

"So did I," William answered before turning to Luke. "As you can see, permission has been granted by all concerned parties for us to see the deed. I suggest you show it to us at once."

"But you are not a lawyer—"

"At once, Mr. Syms."

Luke glared at William for a moment as though he planned to object once more. The ominous look on William's face seemed to change his mind. Luke disappeared into the house.

Lavonia asked Helen, "So, you were not aware that Philemon Midas bought our house?"

"Mais non," she huffed. "As my husband so aptly stated, there is no need for a woman to concern herself with business affairs."

"And he did not realize Philemon Midas was Dr. Amory's benefactor?"

To her surprise, William jumped to Luke's defense. "There was no reason for him to know, Miss Penn. We are not acquainted to the degree that he would be apprised of my personal affairs. I feel confident Mr. Syms has played no part in any intrigue."

"Merci." Helen shot Lavonia a withering look.

At that moment, Luke returned, deed in hand. "Is this what you wanted to see?"

William eagerly took it. "Yes." Skimming its contents, William's gaze finally rested on the signature. But upon examining the name, he shook his head. "This is not the signature of Philemon Midas."

"It is not?" Lavonia couldn't conceal her astonishment.

"If not, then whose could it be?" Luke wondered aloud.

"Could there be another Philemon Midas?" Helen conjectured.

"I have tried to find him twice, with no success. I turned over every stone in Dover years ago, and again this past week, and could not find even one man named Philemon Midas." William shook his head. "No, that could not be possible."

Luke ventured another guess. "Could your benefactor be the father you never knew?"

The hypothesis left William visibly shaken. Seeing his distress, Lavonia placed a comforting hand on his arm.

"Perhaps that is the answer!" Helen agreed.

Casting a gaze upward to William's face, Lavonia asked, "May I tell them?"

He nodded.

"Philemon Midas cannot be his father. His father has been dead for several years."

Luke arched an eyebrow. "And how do you know that?"

"I anticipated I might need these." Reaching into his vest pocket, he withdrew an envelope, yellowed with age. The orphanage address had been scrawled in a sloppy hand with pompous capital letters. "My father's script in no way matches the signature on the deed."

At that instant, Lavonia met with a sudden realization.

"Let me see the signature on the deed."

Though Luke had a puzzled expression, he complied. A quick glance at the writing confirmed what she suspected. She showed the document to everyone else. "Note how the dot on the letter 'i' appears leftward, even though the words slant to the right."

"That is indeed odd," Luke agreed.

"And do you see the extra curl on the loop in the 'P'?"

Helen snatched the paper from Lavonia's grasp. "Why, I recognize that handwriting. It belongs to Uncle Joseph!" With her eyes wide and jaw dropped, she was the picture of surprise. "So he was the one who bought your house?"

"For thousands of pounds less than its market value," Lavonia noted.

"We shall be seeing him about that matter," William said, the determination in his eyes telling her that justice would be served.

Luke smirked at William. "No wonder their uncle can afford to be a benefactor to poor, lost little orphans."

Though he didn't speak, Lavonia saw rage rising in William. Straightening himself to his full height, he looked down at the diminutive Luke. "That may be Joseph Penn's signature, but I assure you, he was not my benefactor." He pulled out a second letter. "The man who wrote this letter was my benefactor."

William flung open the letter and held it up for everyone's perusal. As soon as they saw the precise handwriting, Helen, Katherine, and Lavonia let out a collective gasp. Exchanging looks, they communicated their astonishment to each other without words.

Helen shook her head. "I would not have believed it, had I not seen the evidence with my own eyes."

"Nor I," agreed Katherine. "But there is no doubt in my mind who wrote that letter."

Lavonia's heart raced. *If my father deemed William worthy*

of his benevolence, then he could see what Helen and Luke
fail to admit. That William is indeed worthy, in every way
that matters. Surely, Lord, she prayed, *this must be a sign*
that You intend William for me. Surely I would not be wrong
to listen to my heart!

Luke's voice interrupted her joyous contemplation. "Who
wrote it? And what does this letter prove?"

"I know that handwriting better than my own." Lavonia
answered. "Philemon Midas was my father."

"Your father?" Luke turned to his wife. "Helen, tell your
cousin how preposterous her assumption is."

"But she is right," Helen answered. "I knew my uncle's
handwriting well. He corresponded with our family for many
years, until the time of his death. The letter Dr. Amory holds
in his hand was indeed written by Lavonia's father."

William didn't bother to conceal his shock. "So, your
father was the person who showed me such kindness all
these years?"

Lavonia nodded.

"If only I could have known. I so wanted to thank him."

"He did not seek gratitude, or recognition. He sought only
to serve the Lord. Do you know what his favorite passage
was? Matthew 6:3–4: 'But when thou doest alms, let not thy
left hand know what thy right hand doeth: That thine alms
may be in secret: and thy Father which seeth in secret himself shall reward thee openly.' "

A strange look crossed William's features. "Then that
explains why he sent me this along with the letter." From a
coat pocket, he retrieved a silver money clip and placed it
in Lavonia's hand. Engraved on the clip was, "To William,
As you graduate. P.M." Underneath the initials appeared,
"Matthew 6:3–4."

Staring at the clip, Lavonia remained silent, too filled with
emotion to speak.

"I wish I could somehow repay your father for everything he did for me," William whispered.

"You already do, by using your knowledge to help others," Lavonia answered.

"Including Katherine," Helen interjected.

Lavonia nodded, realizing that Helen's admission signaled a shift in her opinion of William.

"My small contribution barely begins to repay him." William's voice was soft.

"Never let one moment of worry vex you, William." Lavonia couldn't stop the tears that fell on her cheeks. "Our heavenly Father will repay him abundantly."

His violet eyes sparkling, William took hold of her hand. "I know not what I did right, but my heavenly Father has already rewarded me."

"And me as well." Though she focused on him, from the corner of her eye, she saw the others exit. There would be no more opposition to their love for each other.

"Lavonia, have you no idea how difficult it has been for me to stay away from you?"

"And I, you. But I was following Luke's counsel. He suggested I should not see you again for a time, to determine if in your absence my feelings would change."

"And how do you feel, Lavonia?" He touched her chin with his fingers and whispered. "Are you saying you feel as I do?"

"And how is that?"

"I love you. I loved you from the first moment I saw you. The prospect of life without you is too dismal to imagine."

Lavonia felt a shiver tingle up her spine. How she had wanted to hear such words! How she wished she could go away with him, never to think about the past again. But she could not. "But I have promised Aunt Amelia I would go and live in London with her. My stage leaves tomorrow."

"Then I shall follow you to London. I shall follow you to

the edge of the world, if I must." Taking her delicate hands in his strong ones, he brought them up to his chest, placing them just over his beating heart. "As long as you will have me."

"Do you really mean that, William?" she whispered, awed to be living her fantasy.

"I have never meant anything with more sincerity in all my life."

She felt her eyes become misty with emotion. Her heart singing, she felt the chains of bondage breaking as she realized with shining clarity that the Lord had sent William to her. "Nothing would give me more joy."

This time, when he kissed her, Lavonia knew she need not be ashamed.

epilogue

Two Years Later

Stepping onto the porch of the modest white frame house situated in Savannah, Lavonia inhaled deeply the fresh Georgia air. Strong rays of sunlight peeked through tall pines, warming her to the core. Though surviving summer in the southern colony had required some adjustment, Lavonia reveled in the experience of prolonged hot weather. Allowing herself a satisfied sigh after a morning spent writing letters, she smoothed her house dress fashioned in a lightweight, though modestly styled, white cotton.

Two older women greeted her as they passed. "Good morning, Mrs. Amory."

"Good morning, Mrs. Simpson. Mrs. Bailey." She smiled. "Remember our Bible study this afternoon. Four o'clock sharp."

As they nodded their promise to attend, Lavonia sent a silent prayer of thanks to the Lord for the opportunity to teach His word. Since she had started the Bible study that past autumn, attendance had grown from three women to twenty and counting.

"Yoo hoo!" Jane shouted from her backyard, just a few houses down the street.

Lavonia waved to her friend, who was hanging out nightshirts and dressing gowns of varying sizes to dry. She was grateful that she could be so near her friend, so that she was still able to help with the children's lessons as she and Jane had planned.

Jane smiled happily. Her husband had agreed to move to Savannah, and the comforts the city afforded, after their seventh child was born. As was evident by her expanding belly, Jane would be welcoming another new life in a few months.

The sound of her own infant's crying as he awakened from his nap caused Lavonia to notice that the sun was high. Retreating to the indoors, she hastened to the crib. She picked up Willie and held him to her chest, swaying her shoulders to rock him as she stepped toward the kitchen. Her motions resulted in a less urgent cry, but tiny sniffles indicated he was still eager for his meal.

She smiled, bringing her nose to his. "I need no alarm clock with you around, now do I?"

Willie had just finished eating when his father arrived home, a welcome breeze stirring as William opened the door. "And how is my beautiful little family?"

Lavonia turned to answer her husband. It didn't matter that they were no longer considered newlyweds. Her heart beat with as much intensity upon the sight of him as on the day they took each other as man and wife. "We are just wonderful, now that you are home."

Before he could answer, Lavonia heard a small squeal of protest before a piglet jumped out of William's arms and began running around the house.

She let out a shriek. "William! Get that pig out of here!" She eyed a nearby stack of Bibles destined for delivery to the remote wilderness, and her anxiety grew. "That animal will ruin the Bibles!"

Thrilled by the unexpected drama, Willie giggled.

"I think Willie's enjoying the show." William nonetheless began chasing the animal, finally catching her when she made the mistake of running into a far corner.

Letting out an audible sigh of relief that the Bibles and the rest of the house remained unharmed, Lavonia placed her

free hand on her chest and shook her head. "Payment for services rendered, I assume?"

William nodded.

"Why ever did you bring that animal in here?"

"I wanted to show Willie." Coming closer to Lavonia, he
held up the pig for his son to see. "What do you think of this
pig, Willie? Can you say 'pig'?"

Having not yet uttered his first word, the baby smiled and
swatted his hand toward the animal.

"Unless you have developed a sudden aversion to sausage
and bacon, I suggest we not encourage Willie to adopt the
piglet as a household pet."

"Oh, all right," he answered with mock disappointment.
"Before I neglect to tell you, I stopped by the general store
as I promised. The fabric you ordered has been delayed. Mr.
Watson said it most likely will not arrive for several more
months."

"Jane and I shall never begin our quilts!"

"If winter arrives before the fabric, you can bundle up
Willie and walk to her house for a sewing session every day,
if you like. You can quilt while her children write their
lessons."

"Indeed." Lavonia let out a sigh. "Still, I miss the ability to
purchase fabrics whenever I please."

"Speaking of what we miss," William said, pulling a letter
from his trouser pocket with his free hand, "this arrived
today."

"Oh, a letter from Kitty!"

"I know you have been anxious to hear from her." Handing
her the letter, he took advantage of their closeness to steal a
soft kiss, a habit she found endearing. "I shall introduce my
little friend here to her new home in the pig pen while you
catch up on all the news. Enjoy."

"I already have," she teased.

As soon as William left, she looked into the little face of the infant she held. "Would you like to hear all about the news of your Auntie Kitty?"

Willie cooed his consent, but heavy eyelids told a different story. After kissing the top of his head, she opened the letter and began reading:

Dear Vonnie:

Bonjour! Comment allez-vous aujourd'hui?

Such a lovely day today here. Nice and cool. How do you endure the heat you describe? Such abominable sweltering would no doubt be enough to require me to take to my bed.

Helen and Luke continue to be exemplary hosts even though Helen has stopped eating breakfast and complains that her stomach feels as turbulent as the Atlantic during a hurricane. I do wonder what causes her maladies.

Received word from Aunt Amelia. You would have enjoyed her letter. She is still quite the partygoer, although now she mentions church activities as well. She did report that she finally recovered the part of her fortune Uncle Joseph embezzled. He would admit to no wrongdoing, but she wrote to us that, because of her Christian principles, she sought not revenge, but simply the money to which she was entitled. Personally, I do not see why we did not throw him into prison, where he belongs! I do hope he is grateful for our generosity in not prosecuting him, but I harbor little hope he is capable of such emotion. That he used our dear father's alias in the signing of that deed—his treachery was truly ironic, don't you agree?

We see nothing of Uncle Joseph now. Because William's solicitor was so successful in convincing him to return the money he stole from us, Uncle Joseph refuses to speak to

*any of the family except through his own solicitor. I heard
a rumor that he and his dreadful wife are living abroad. I
assume her fortune pays their expenses.*

Osmond received word yesterday that the latest opening in London was filled by another clergyman even
younger than he. Osmond is convinced that this clergyman used his family connections to obtain the post
unfairly. He is quite depressed. In fact, he has abandoned all hope of ever moving to London.

Nevertheless, our courtship continues. He comes to
call each Tuesday and Friday evening, always arriving
in time for dinner. And of course, he escorts me to
church each Sunday morning for worship. I have taken
to occupying a place in the front pew, as is natural since
the quite colossal bejeweled ring he presented me with
upon the occasion of our betrothal is tangible evidence
of my position. Simply everyone attended the gala Helen
and Luke hosted to honor the occasion, so even without
the ring, there should be no doubt about our status
among those who matter. Still, the ring is lovely, and I
must confess, I do anticipate Sunday mornings greatly
since we agreed to wed. I often feel as though Osmond is
speaking only to me with his eloquent sermons!

The only detriment to this pleasant arrangement is
that Osmond insists we decide on a date for our nup-
tials. But how can I marry without you being present as
my matron of honor, Vonnie? I have made clear to him
that you simply cannot bring little Willie on such an
arduous journey. Vraiment, what would we do should
any ill befall you because of us? I would never forgive
myself. When I remind him of this obvious fact, Osmond
is understanding. I confess that at times his prodding
can be tiresome. Upon those occasions, I am forced to
retire to my bedchamber, an event he prefers to avoid

since it shortens his visits with me.

Osmond will soon be coming to call, so I must bid you au revoir! *Do write soon!*

With love,
Kitty

Post Script: We just found a new doctor to replace William.

Sighing, Lavonia replaced the letter in its envelope.

Willie was sleeping soundly in her arms, his rhythmic breathing a comfort to her. As she stroked his chubby cheek, a sunbeam reflected off the simple band engraved with *Vous et nul autre* that William had given her on their wedding day.

The voice of the one she loved interrupted her musings. "*Vous et nul autre*. You and no other." Coming closer, William knelt by the side of her rocker. Taking her left hand in his, he studied the ring. "Those words mean more to me than ever. And to think that I almost lost you."

She gazed into the eyes of the man she married. "We certainly struggled with the Lord's plan for us, did we not?"

William smiled back at her. "Thankfully, He persisted."

"Yes. Thankfully."

Stirring from his nap, Willie's eyes blinked until they were open. Smiling at his parents, he cooed three syllables. Laughing, William and Lavonia wondered if their little boy was trying to say "thankfully," too.

A Letter To Our Readers

Dear Reader:

In order that we might better contribute to your reading enjoyment, we would appreciate your taking a few minutes to respond to the following questions. We welcome your comments and read each form and letter we receive. When completed, please return to the following:

Rebecca Germany, Fiction Editor
Heartsong Presents
PO Box 719
Uhrichsville, Ohio 44683

1. Did you enjoy reading *Destinations?*
   ☐ Very much. I would like to see more books
     by this author!
   ☐ Moderately
     I would have enjoyed it more if _____

     _____

     _____

2. Are you a member of **Heartsong Presents**? Yes ☐ No ☐
   If no, where did you purchase this book?_____

   _____

3. How would you rate, on a scale from 1 (poor) to 5 (superior), the cover design?_____

4. On a scale from 1 (poor) to 10 (superior), please rate the following elements.

   _____ Heroine   _____ Plot

   _____ Hero   _____ Inspirational theme

   _____ Setting   _____ Secondary characters

5. These characters were special because_____

_____

_____

6. How has this book inspired your life?_____

_____

_____

7. What settings would you like to see covered in future
   Heartsong Presents books?_____

_____

_____

8. What are some inspirational themes you would like to see
   treated in future books?_____

_____

_____

9. Would you be interested in reading other **Heartsong
   Presents** titles?   Yes ❏   No ❏

10. Please check your age range:
    ❏ Under 18   ❏ 18-24   ❏ 25-34
    ❏ 35-45   ❏ 46-55   ❏ Over 55

11. How many hours per week do you read?_____

Name _____

Occupation _____

Address _____

City _____ State _____ Zip _____

Greece. . .a land of historic enchantment and romance. . . a perfect place for love. From the pen of Melanie Panagiotopoulos, a resident of Athens, come four thrilling love stories. . .

Savor the charm of Greece through these four unique stories. Experience the search for the ultimate gift of love—between a man and a woman and from the God whose gifts are good and perfect.

paperback, 464 pages, 5 ³⁄₁₆" x 8"

❤ ❤ ❤ ❤ ❤ ❤ ❤ ❤ ❤ ❤ ❤ ❤ ❤ ❤ ❤ ❤

❤ ❤ ❤ ❤ ❤ ❤ ❤ ❤ ❤ ❤ ❤ ❤ ❤ ❤ ❤ ❤

·······Presents·······